Incest

Marquis de Sade

Translated by Andrew Brown

ALMA CLASSICS

ALMA CLASSICS LTD
London House
243-253 Lower Mortlake Road
Richmond
Surrey TW9 2LL
United Kingdom
www.almaclassics.com

Incest first published in French in 1799
This translation first published by Hesperus Press Ltd in 2003
This edition first published by Alma Classics Ltd in 2013

Translation and Introduction © Andrew Brown, 2003, 2013
Cover image © Francesco Pelosi

Printed in Great Britain by CPI Group (UK) Ltd, Croydon, CR0 4YY

ISBN: 978-1-84749-297-5

Contents

Introduction v

Incest 1

Note on the Text 108

Introduction

"Lolita, light of my life, fire of my loins. My sin, my soul."
"You will always be my favourite, Eugénie; you will be the
angel and the light of my life, the fire of my soul, my reason
for living."

The first is Humbert Humbert's description of his
nymphet stepdaughter. The second is Franval's address to
his real daughter: not yet fourteen but soon to be "sacrificed" – apparently willingly – to his desires.

Both Nabokov, in *Lolita*, and de Sade, in *Incest* (whose
French title, less tendentiously, is simply *Eugénie de Franval*),
are – as the ardent language of their protagonists shows –
narrating love stories. Both are focusing on what we know
to be the hellish world of child abuse. And both under-
gird their stories with more or less fraught and inchoate
apologias for sexually transgressive behaviour – aesthetic
transfiguration in Humbert's case; a radical critique of
social conventions in that of Franval. Both their narratives
are "composed" in prison (de Sade actually wrote *Incest*
in the Bastille, where he had been incarcerated for sexual
malpractice, while Nabokov's protagonist Humbert is await-
ing trial for the murder of Lolita's ex-lover Quilty), and in

both stories there is a critical subtext arguing that social norms can themselves be a form of symbolic incarceration.

However monstrously self-serving Humbert's language may be, and however much he comes – belatedly and with considerable crocodilian sentimentality – to see that he has robbed Lolita of her childhood, he seems at times an outsider; to have more moral insight into the strange mixture of innocence and corruption that is American society, with its fetishistic cult of youth and its denial of the paedophilia that sometimes lurks within this, than most of the people around him.

In de Sade, if you want an example of a sexually exploitative, "unnatural" practice in thrall to male power, where the fate of young women is decided for them, you need look no further than marriage. For if there is an emancipatory moment in de Sade's story, it lies in the fact that Eugénie defiantly refuses the suitors arranged for her by her mother. Admittedly this is because of her own incestuous love for her father – while the extent to which Eugénie has been programmed into incest by that father is an open question. By isolating Eugénie from her mother and ensuring that he will be the only adult who really counts for her, Franval has nonetheless ensured that she is given an unusually all-round education; he has told her of the prevalent social norms that condemn incest and encouraged her to reject his advances if there is someone she prefers to him. Her relative isolation makes her something of an *enfant sauvage*, albeit an unusually civilized one, and of course it is unlikely that Franval will paint the conventions of his society in a particularly appealing light. But Franval at least waits until his daughter is an adolescent before, in one of de Sade's theatrical and ritualistic set pieces, deflowering her. Not all child abusers show such restraint. In any case, in de Sade's society, young women were married off early: Madame de Farneille is seventeen when she gives birth to her daughter, and Franval's wife is, in turn, only sixteen and a half when she presents her husband with a daughter, Eugénie.

In fact, it is not clear that either Nabokov or de Sade are all that interested in incest as such. For Humbert, certainly, Lolita is important more as a nymphet than a stepdaughter. As for de Sade, he adumbrates the concept that incest is merely one more example of the urge to transgress that is the dominant impulse of the Sadeian world. A more important theme might well be the murder of the mother, for in both stories, one very real victim is indeed the daughter's mother. In *Lolita*, Charlotte Haze is treated as a banal, clinging, vaguely pathetic figure by the narrator. In *Incest*, Mme de Franval is forced to endure both mental and physical cruelty. We tend to think, in patriarchy, of the father embodying the authority of law, and the mother as a more "natural" figure, but here the father is the transgressor and the voice of a putatively repressed nature. The mother becomes the symbol of the law which both Humbert and Franval flout – the usual division of labour between nature and culture is disturbed – and in *Incest*, at least, it is notable that Franval repents more for his offence against his wife than for that against his daughter.

Franval's sequestering of Eugénie mirrors Enlightenment experiments designed to determine where nature ends and culture begins. He wants to find out whether his daughter will feel a natural aversion to incest with him, or whether such aversion is "merely" the product of the prejudices of a particular society. The text repeatedly applies the words "philosophical" and "system" to Franval: these were, in the eighteenth century, code words for the unorthodox speculations of the *philosophes* critical of the Church and the *ancien régime*, and eager to "change the common way of thinking", as Diderot said of the *Encyclopédie*. The word "libertine" meant both a freethinker and a dissolute character: it was assumed that anyone who disbelieved in the threats and promises of the Gospel would have no fear of retribution and would inevitably yield to every conceivable temptation. De Sade's protagonists, including Franval, go one further, and set out systematically to transgress all the moral injunctions of Christianity, and then all moral injunctions *tout court*. Sometimes in de Sade this leads to transgression itself imploding: since transgression requires a law to transgress, it is thus dependent on that law, and once the injunction to transgress becomes so urgent, transgression itself becomes a new law. In any case, transgression in de Sade is not always merely negative: it can be a way of obeying a law higher than that of human conventions, namely nature.

In so far as *Incest* is a *conte philosophique*, its heart is the dialogue between Franval and the priest Clervil. The priest has to face several arguments set out by Franval in his defence of incest. First, there is nothing good or bad but thinking makes it so: nature is neutral and only human beings attribute value to it (by decreeing, for instance, that one conjugation of sexual organs is licit and another abhorrent). Second, all human actions are determined by a power which may be good or bad, but to which we have to submit, since in this submission alone resides our happiness – a version of one stoic argument, which tends to promote the virtue of *ataraxia* or indifference (why make such a fuss about a trivial little thing like incest?). Third, all happiness is relative: the priest is happy being a priest; Franval is happy living incestuously with his daughter; who is to decide between them?

At this point the priest counters with the "voice of conscience": Franval must surely suffer qualms because of his wrongdoing. A more decided Sadeian hero would retort that his greatest pleasure lay precisely in deliberately disobeying the "tyrannical" and "arbitrary" voice of conscience; Franval's response is less forthright, and consists in once more adducing the notion of ethical relativity. If conscience were a sure guide, it would say the same thing in all times and all places. This is manifestly not so, he claims: what is done with impunity in France is punishable in Japan.

The priest's counter-argument runs like this: it may be that human beings in different cultures have different laws; it may even be that the taboo on incest is not universal (he suggests that father-daughter marriages are permitted "on the banks of the Ganges"). But all cultures have laws, and the human beings who belong to that culture must obey its legal code even if they are aware that another culture thinks differently. This argument squares the circle as between relativism (laws are particular to cultures and have no necessary validity outside them) and universalism (there is one human nature and there should ultimately be one set of laws for the entire human race).

Clervil's compromise solution is capable of more sophisticated formulations, but even as it stands it melds together law, with its universalizing momentum, and custom, with its particularism; it takes adequate account of our sense that human cultures are startlingly diverse, while refusing to collapse into mere ethical relativism. But it is an uneasy compromise, an unstable synthesis of law and custom. Our inability to decide how to distinguish between these – how to attribute to law a dignity superior to that of "mere" custom if it is not granted that law can be transcendentally founded (as in a revealed religion) nor deduced on grounds of pure rationality (since it seems that reason too has a history and a geography) – render all of Clervil's arguments vulnerable.

Once Humbert Humbert has murdered his rival Quilty, he decides that "since I had disregarded all laws of humanity, I might as well disregard the rules of traffic"; he drives away from the scene of his crime on the wrong side of the road, and passes through all the red lights until the police cars finally catch up. We want to say that Humbert's exploitation of Lolita and his murder of Quilty are on a different level from his infractions of the Highway Code, just as we want to say that Clervil's example of the Parisian boulevards ignores our very real sense that some crimes are more serious than others. De Sade too sometimes experiments with an antinomianism that seems like an act of exasperated resentment against the moral perfectionism expressed in the Epistle of James ("For whosoever shall keep the whole law, and yet offend in one point, he is guilty of all"); the "slippery slope" argument voiced by Clervil to enforce total submission to all society's laws is ironically endorsed in *Incest*, where sexual transgression leads to murder, uxoricide and matricide. We also want to say that there is at least a relative universality, a rationale, behind the varying customs of different societies: drive on the wrong side of the road and you risk killing someone. Likewise, de Sade sometimes appeals to nature as that which transcends cultural difference. Franval and his daughter have already rejected the claims of custom (whose other name is "prejudice"): rather than seeing the relative rationality of different customs, Franval rejects the claims of custom, as such, in the name of a nature that lies beyond.

But "nature" is one of the most complex words in de Sade. Nature is "what happens"; blind and mechanical; humans should learn to live with its cold, impersonal grandeur. Nature is benevolent, the source of all life and all the pleasures associated with it, specifically sex; humans should enjoy these pleasures while they can. (It is religion which, by regulating sexuality, is unnatural – much more unnatural than incest.) Nature is malevolent: as eruptive as a volcano, as cruel as the tiger when it tears its prey to pieces. Humans should mimic its destructive power.

Though neither Clervil nor Franval are nominalist enough to say so, "nature" is in any case a culturally conditioned construction: it is posited as what must be beyond all customs, and only a realization of the variety of those customs allows us to separate custom from law, or culture from nature, in the first place. In its scientific sense, nature must be universal (the laws of gravity, if not marriage arrangements, must be the same on the banks of the Ganges as they are by the Seine), and yet that universality is precarious and revisable: Newton is corrected by Einstein, "scientific" theories (Darwinism, Freudianism) may over time reveal more about the people and the societies that produced and consumed them than about nature as such.

The arguments put forward by Franval to justify incest fail in two main ways, and they both involve the fragile notions of autonomy and universality. Franval's incest is ultimately an act of self-assertion: its subtext is "my desires will brook no restraint". Only when the self-assertion of others intrudes on his own (when he is robbed of his money and left to wander half-naked through the forest) is he forced to review the values by which he has lived his life, to realize that autonomy is necessarily limited. And his philosophizing, which glorifies self-assertion by an appeal to the authority of nature – the subtext here being "I serve nature alone, and like all natural beings I seek solely my own power and pleasure" – denies his heteronomous dependence on others: on the submissiveness of Eugénie, first and foremost; and on the fact that it is only because of others – because the customs of the Hottentots and the Japanese are different from those of the French – that he can have any inkling of the nature he claims to serve. He cannot know this nature unaided, or by mere introspection; nature as self-assertive desire is his own interpretation, not fact. And this is ultimately where the positions of Clervil and Franval turn into mirror images of each other: they universalize and eternalize what is limited in time and space.

Even Clervil, well aware of the cultural variability of custom, fails to realize that the human mind cannot rest in mere pluralistic acquiescence: in comparing what is done on the banks of the Seine with what is done on the banks of the Ganges, we necessarily evaluate the two sets of practices; this is why customs change. What was a capital offence in de Sade's society is so no longer (indeed, it is only because laws change, perhaps partly thanks to de Sade, that we can now read de Sade).

Clervil is right to see that a culture is a complex network of rights and obligations in which any one transgression risks unravelling the whole skein, but he is wrong in deducing the theocratic totalitarianist position that all laws are therefore set in stone. He is ultimately a monist, worshipping the way things are (though his acceptance of the penitent Franval makes him a more sympathetic figure and suggests a more subtle and adaptable position). So is Franval, though he views the way things are differently from Franval: he wishes to conform not to law but to nature. They both deny that human beings are essentially counter-factual creatures, always able to transcend the way things are, by whatever name we call that "given". If there is a given we are never obliged to accept it. We can imagine things being different; we can invent stories: such as *Incest*, which is, after all, a story as well as a debate.

It is true that it is a rather dry story at times, though it does at least end in satisfyingly Gothic gloom – dungeons and castles, thunder and lightning, robbers galloping away, improbable coincidences and belated repentances, a torch-lit funeral – all very operatic (you can almost hear the music: by Verdi). But it also ends on the outskirts of that Sadeian location par excellence, the Black Forest. It is in the Black Forest that de Sade sets the capital of his dark empire, the isolated castle of Silling, where the debauchees of the *120 Days of Sodom* indulge in the torture of their victims, far from the restraints of culture and, so they claim, in the name of the way things are (here: sexual desire, in all its ramifications).

Why not yield, opportunistically (sadistically, perhaps), to the opportunism of geographical accident and recall that it was in the Black Forest, from his mountain hut at Todtnauberg (its very name makes it sound like a Golgotha of the spirit), that the German philosopher Martin Heidegger, from beginning to end of the Nazi regime, issued the fateful directives of fundamental ontology. The monstrosities complicitously catalogued by de Sade in the *120 Days of Sodom*, and adumbrated in *Incest*, share at least one deep tendency with the philosophy of Heidegger: on the one hand we have the denigration of "culture", that delicate symbolic network of human relations that human beings are always free to revise and correct, and on the other the exaltation of "the way things are". Called, by the one, "Nature", in all its amoral (and thus immoral) power; and by the other, "Being".

– Andrew Brown

Incest

To educate man and to improve his morals: that is the sole objective of this anecdote. The reader should be imbued with a sense of the great peril that perpetually dogs the footsteps of those who permit themselves everything when satisfying their desires. May they come to realize that a good upbringing, wealth, talent and the gifts bestowed by Nature only serve to lead one astray – if these qualities are not borne up and made worthy by restraint, good behaviour, wisdom and modesty – these are the very truths which we are here going to prove. May we be forgiven the monstrous details of the dreadful crime we are obliged to recount: is it possible to arouse a detestation of such aberrations when one is not brave enough to depict them in all their nakedness?

It is rare that everything should be so harmoniously organized in one person as to bring him to prosperity. Is he favoured by Nature? If so, Fortune refuses her gifts. Does Fortune shower her favours on him? Then Nature is bound to have maltreated him. It seems that the hand of Heaven has decided to demonstrate, in each individual as in its most sublime operations, that the laws of equilibrium are the foremost laws of the universe – the laws which simultaneously govern all events, and all vegetable and animal life.

Franval, who lived in Paris, where he was born, possessed not only an income of four hundred thousand livres but also the most handsome figure, the most agreeable features and the most varied talents. But beneath this outwardly seductive surface all the vices were concealed, sadly including those which, once adopted and made habitual, lead rapidly to crime. An imagination disordered to a degree impossible to describe was Franval's main failing – one that can never be overcome, since a diminution of its power simply increases the strength of its effects; the less they are capable of, the more they try to do; the less they act, the more they have recourse to invention; each age brings new ideas, and satiety, far from cooling their ardour, merely leads to more deadly refinements.

As we have said, the charms of youth and all the talents that enhance it were possessed in profusion by Franval, but given that he held moral and religious duties in the deepest contempt, it proved impossible for his teachers to make him adopt any of them.

In a century when the most dangerous books come into the hands of children as easily as into those of their fathers and their guardians, when reckless systematizing can pass itself off as philosophy, unbelief as strength of mind and libertinage for imagination, the wit shown by young Franval merely aroused laughter; one minute he was being scolded for it, and the next praised. Franval's father, who favoured modish sophisms, was the first to encourage his son to think *sensibly* about all these things; he himself lent him the works which could corrupt him most quickly; what tutor would have dared, after that, to inculcate principles different from those of the house in which he was obliged to please his masters?

In any case, Franval lost his parents when he was still very young, and at the age of nineteen, an old uncle, who himself died shortly afterwards, made over to him, as soon as he was to be married, all the possessions that were destined one day to belong to him.

M. de Franval, with such a fortune, was bound to find it easy to get married. Countless possible candidates presented themselves, but as he had begged his uncle to give him a girl younger than himself – one bringing as few companions as possible – his old kinsman, aiming to satisfy his nephew, let his choice fall on a certain Mademoiselle de Farneille, daughter of a financier, now with only her mother left alive; still young, it was true, but with an income of sixty thousand solid livres; fifteen years old, and with the most delightful features in the whole of Paris at that time... She had one of those virginal faces in which sincerity and affability are both clearly visible through the delicate features of Love and all the Graces... lovely blond hair rippling down to her waist, big blue eyes suffused with tenderness and modesty, a slender, supple and delicate figure, skin like a lily and as fresh as a rose, possessing many talents and a vivid but somewhat wistful imagination, with some of that gentle melancholy which leads one to love books and solitude – all attributes which Nature seems to grant only to the individuals for whom it is keeping unhappiness in store, as if to make that happiness seem less bitter when they encounter it, imbuing them at such times with a sombre and affecting voluptuousness and making them prefer tears to the frivolous joys of happiness, which are much less powerful and much less intense.

Mme de Farneille, thirty-two years old at the time of her daughter's marriage, was also a woman of intelligence and charm, but inclined perhaps a little too much to strictness and reserve. Desirous of the happiness of her only child, she had consulted the whole of Paris on this marriage, and as she no longer had any relatives and, if she needed advice, only a few of those cold-hearted friends to whom everything is a matter of indifference, she was persuaded that the young man who was being proposed for her daughter was, without a doubt, the best person she could possibly find in Paris, and that she would commit an unforgivable folly if she failed to take advantage of this opportunity. So the marriage took place, and the young couple, wealthy enough to move into their own house, settled into it in the days following their wedding.

None of those vices of fickleness, disorderly conduct or empty-headedness which prevent a man from being fully grown by the time he is thirty had entered young Franval's heart; on the best of terms with himself, a devotee of order and well versed in the arts of managing a house, Franval had, as far as this aspect of life's happiness was concerned, all the necessary qualities. His vices, of an entirely different kind, were much more the failings of maturity than the products of scatterbrained youth: artfulness, intrigue... malevolence, a black heart, egotism, a great deal of cunning and deceit and, to cast a veil over all this, not only the grace and talents we have mentioned, but eloquence, a sharp mind and the most seductive outward manners one could imagine. This was the man we have to depict.

Mlle de Farneille, who, as was customary, had known her husband for at most a month before tying her destiny to his, was deceived by this false glitter and became its dupe. The days were not long enough for her to indulge in the pleasure of gazing at him; she idolized him, and things had gone so far that people might have feared the worst for this young woman if any obstacles had come to disturb the sweet and even course of a marriage in which she found, she said, the only happiness of her life.

As for Franval, philosophical when it came to women as indeed about everything else in life, he considered this charming person with a fine show of indifference.

"The woman who belongs to us," he would say, "is a kind of individual whom usage enslaves to us; she has to be yielding, submissive... perfectly sensible: not that I take much account of the prejudices of dishonour that a wife can bring on us when she imitates our misbehaviour – it is merely that it is not pleasant when someone else takes it into her head to steal our privileges; all the rest is perfectly unimportant, and adds nothing to our happiness."

With a husband who feels that way, it is easy to foresee that the unfortunate woman who is to be bound to him in matrimony cannot expect her path to be strewn with roses. Decent, sensitive, well-brought-up and impelled by love to anticipate all the desires of the only man in the world who occupied her thoughts, Mme de Franval carried her chains through the first few years without even suspecting the extent of her enslavement; it was obvious enough to her that she was merely gleaning in the fields of marriage, but she was still made happy enough by what was left to her, and all her zeal and her greatest attention were devoted to ensuring, in these short moments granted to her affection, that Franval would find at the least everything she thought necessary for the happiness of her darling husband.

The most conclusive of all the proofs that Franval did not always stray from his duty, however, was the fact that in the very first year of his marriage, his wife, now sixteen and a half, gave birth to a daughter even more beautiful than her mother, whom the father immediately called Eugénie... Eugénie, at once the horror and the miracle of nature.

M. de Franval, who, the minute this child saw the light of day, no doubt conceived the most detestable designs on her, straight away separated her from her mother. Until the age of seven, Eugénie was looked after by women who

Franval could be sure of, and who, limiting themselves to encouraging the development of a pleasant temperament and to teaching her how to read, deliberately refrained from giving her any knowledge of the religious or moral principles about which a girl of that age is commonly supposed to be instructed.

Mme de Farneille and her daughter, deeply shocked by this behaviour, complained to M. de Franval, who replied with indifference that his plan was to make his daughter happy, and so he did not wish to inculcate chimerical notions into her, as their sole effect is to frighten people without ever being of any use to them; it was best if such a daughter, whose only need was to learn how to please others, remained ignorant of such silly nonsense, the fantastical existence of which would trouble her peace of mind without adding either a single extra truth to her moral being or a single extra grace to her physical appearance. Such comments met with the loftiest disapproval of Mme de Farneille, who was drawing nearer to thoughts of heaven the further she drew away from the pleasures of this world: devoutness is a weakness that affects particular ages and particular states of health. Amid the tumult of the passions, a future which seems far away rarely causes much anxiety, but when those passions cease to speak so loud... when we draw near life's end... when everything, finally, abandons us, we throw ourselves back onto the mercy of the God we heard about in childhood, and if, from a philosophical point of view, these second illusions are just as fantastical as the others, they are, at least, not so dangerous.

Franval's mother-in-law had no relatives, little credit of her own to draw upon, and at the most, as we have said, just a few of those fair-weather friends who soon melt away if we need their help. Finding herself struggling against an amiable, young, well-placed son-in-law, she decided sensibly enough that it would be simpler to content herself with a few mild reprimands, rather than having recourse to more vigorous measures against a man who would ruin the mother and have the daughter locked up if anyone dared to cross swords with him: for this reason, she merely hazarded a few critical remarks, and left it at that as soon as she saw that it was all leading nowhere.

Franval, sure of his superiority, and realizing that they were afraid of him, soon lost all restraint in every area of life whatsoever and, barely even troubling to draw a veil over his actions so as to conceal them from the public, he marched straight to his horrible goal.

As soon as Eugénie reached the age of seven, Franval took her to see his wife, and this loving mother – who had not seen her child since giving birth to her – caressed her insatiably, held her pressed tight to her breast for two hours, covered her with kisses and drenched her with her tears. She wanted to know all about her childish talents, but Eugénie had only learnt to read fluently, to enjoy the most robust health and to be as beautiful as the angels. Mme de Franval felt a new despair when she realized that her daughter was truly unaware of even the most elementary principles of religion.

"But Monsieur!" she said to her husband. "Are you giving her an upbringing that is fit merely for this world? Will you not deign to reflect that she is to live in it for a mere instant, like us, before plunging into a dire eternity if you deprive her of what will enable her to enjoy a happier destiny at the feet of the Being from whom she received life?"

"If Eugénie knows nothing, Madame," replied Franval, "if these maxims are carefully hidden from her, she cannot possibly be unhappy; for, if they are true, the Supreme Being is too just to punish her for her ignorance, and if they are false, what need is there to tell her about them? As for the other aspects of her education that need to be taken care of, please trust me: from today I will be her tutor, and I will answer for it that in a few years, your daughter will surpass all the other children of her age."

Mme de Franval persisted. Drawing on the eloquence of her heart to assist that of reason, she shed a few tears: but Franval was quite unmoved by them, and indeed did not seem even to notice them. He had Eugénie taken away, telling his wife that if she took it into her head to put any obstacles, of whatever kind, in the way of the education he intended to give his daughter, or if she tried to suggest principles different from those he planned to instil in her, she would deprive herself of the pleasure of seeing her altogether, and he would send his daughter to one of his chateaux, from which she would never emerge. Mme de Franval, ever submissive, was quiet for a moment; then she begged her husband never to separate her from such a dear possession, and promised, weeping, that she would in no way hinder the education being prepared for her.

From that moment, Mlle de Franval was placed in a very fine apartment, next to that of her father, with a governess of great intelligence, an under-governess, a chambermaid and two little girls of her own age, for her sole amusement. She was given tutors in writing, drawing, poetry, natural history, oratory, geography, astronomy, anatomy, Greek, English, German, Italian, fencing, dancing, riding and music.

Eugénie got up every day at seven o'clock, whatever the season; she ran off to the garden where she breakfasted on a thick hunk of rye bread; she came back at eight, spent a few moments in her father's apartment, where he romped and played with her or taught her little society games; until nine she prepared her homework; then the first tutor arrived; five came in all, until two o'clock. She was served her meal separately, with her two girlfriends and her chief governess; lunch consisted of vegetables, fish, pastries and fruit; there was never any meat, soup, wine, liqueurs or coffee. From three until four Eugénie returned to play in the garden for an hour with her little companions; they practised tennis, ball, skittles, badminton or running races; they wore comfortable clothing, depending on the different seasons; nothing constricted their waists: they were never strapped into those ridiculous whalebone corsets, equally dangerous for stomach and chest, which impede a young girl's breathing and inevitably attack her lungs. From four until six, Mlle de Franval was visited by new tutors, and as not all of them could appear on the same day, the others would come the day after. Three times a week, Eugénie went to see a play with her father, in little private theatre boxes with gratings hired for her use on an annual basis. At nine, she returned home for supper; she was served only vegetables and fruit. From ten to eleven, four times a week, Eugénie played with her servants, read various novels and then went to bed. On the other three days, the ones on which Franval did not dine out, she would spend her time alone in her father's apartment, and this period was taken up with what Franval called his "lectures". In these, he inculcated in his daughter his maxims on morality and religion; he presented to her, on the one hand, what certain men thought on these issues, and on the other he set out what he himself thought.

With her high intelligence, extensive knowledge, alert mind and the passions that were already starting to smoulder within her, it is easy to imagine the progress that such systems made in Eugenie's soul, but as the unworthy Franval was not intent on making her self-assured in mind alone, his lectures rarely ended without inflaming her heart, and this dreadful man had so successfully found the way to please his daughter, he suborned her so artfully, he made himself so useful in her education and her pleasures, he anticipated so promptly and ardently everything that might prove agreeable to her, that Eugénie, even amid the most brilliant social circles, found no one she liked as much as her father, and even before her father expressed his own desires, the weak and innocent creature had developed in her young heart all the feelings of friendship, gratitude and affection which inevitably lead to the most ardent love. She had eyes only for Franval in the whole world; he alone counted for her, and she rebelled at the idea of everything that could separate her from him; she would have lavished on him, not her honour, not her charms – all these sacrifices would have appeared too slight for the cherished object of her idolatry – but her blood, her very life, if this tender soulmate of hers had been capable of asking it of her.

The same could not be said for the feelings Mlle de Franval felt stirring in her heart for her worthy and unhappy mother. Her father, by cleverly telling his daughter that Mme de Franval, as his wife, demanded from him care and attention that often prevented him from doing for his dear Eugénie everything that his heart commanded, had found the secret of stirring up, in the young girl's soul, instead of the various respectful and affectionate emotions that should have arisen for such a mother, hatred and jealousy.

"My friend, my brother," Eugénie would sometimes say to Franval, who did not wish his daughter to use any other expressions when addressing him, "this wife that you call your own, this creature who, so you say, gave birth to me, must be really demanding, since she always wants to have you at her side and thus deprives me of the happiness of spending my life with you… I see it all: you prefer her to your own Eugénie. For my part, I will never love anyone or anything that steals your heart away from me."

"My dear friend," Franval would reply, "no, nobody in the whole wide world will ever obtain such powerful rights over me as you. The bonds that exist between this woman and your best friend – the product of custom and social convention – are something I view philosophically, and they will never outweigh the ties which unite you and me… You will always be my favourite, Eugénie; you will be the angel and the light of my life, the fire of my soul, my reason for living."

"Ah! How sweet those words sound!" replied Eugénie. "Say them again, say them often, my friend… If only you knew how the expressions of your affection gratify me!"

And taking Franval's hand, which she placed on her own heart, she continued:

"Indeed, I can feel all those expressions right here."

"Let your tender caresses assure me of those feelings," replied Franval, pressing her into his arms… And the treacherous man thus completed, without the slightest remorse, his seduction of the unfortunate girl.

But Eugénie was coming up to the age of fourteen: this was the age when Franval planned to consummate his crime. Let us shudder!… The crime was consummated.

The very day she reached that age, or rather the day on which her fourteenth year had been completed, as they both found themselves in the country, without relatives or anyone else to get in the way, the Count, having dressed up his daughter like those virgins who were once consecrated to the temple of Venus, brought her, at eleven o'clock in the morning, into a luxurious drawing room whose windows filtered the daylight through gauze curtains, and whose furnishings were strewn with flowers. A throne of roses had been set up in the middle; Franval led his daughter to it.

"Eugénie," he said, seating her on it, "today you must be the queen of my heart, and allow me to worship you on my knees!"

"You, worship me, my brother, when it is I who owe everything to you, when it is you who have created me and shaped me?... Ah! Let me rather fall at your feet: that is the only place for me, the sole place where I aspire to be with you."

"Oh my tender Eugénie," said the Count, sitting next to her on those seats of flowers that were to serve his victory, "if it is true that you owe anything to me, if the feelings you demonstrate for me are indeed as sincere as you say, do you know what means you can use to convince me of the fact?"

"What means are those, my brother? Tell me, quickly, so that I can make haste to employ them."

"All those charms, Eugénie, that Nature has lavished on you, all the allure with which she beautifies you – all these things you must sacrifice to me on the instant."

"What is this you are asking me? Are you not the master of everything? Does what you have made not belong to you? Can anyone else ever enjoy the work of your hands?"

"But you can imagine the prejudices of men."

"You have never hidden them from me."

"So I do not wish to transgress them without your acceptance."

"Do you not hold them in contempt, as I do?"

"Indeed, but I do not wish to be your tyrant, and even less your seducer; I want the benefits I am seeking to be granted to me out of love alone. You know what society is like; I have never concealed any of its attractions from you: to hide men from your eyes, to let you see no one except myself, would have been a deception unworthy of me. If there is anywhere in the world a single person you prefer to me, name him, now: I will go to the ends of the earth to find him, and bring him straight away to your arms. It is your happiness, in a word, which I am seeking, my angel, your happiness much more than my own; those sweet pleasures that you are able to give me would mean nothing to me, if they were not the price of your love. Decide, then, Eugénie; you are on the point of being sacrificed, and sacrificed you must be, but you yourself must name the sacrificer: I will renounce the pleasures which come with that title, if I cannot obtain them from your soul, and I will always be worthy of your heart. If I am not the person you prefer, I will bring you the man you can cherish, and thus at least I will have earned your affection, even if I have been unable to captivate your heart, and I will be the friend of Eugénie, even if I have not managed to become her lover."

"You will be all of that, my brother, you will be all of that!" said Eugénie, burning with love and desire. "To whom do you think I should sacrifice myself, if not to the only man I love? Who in the whole world can be worthier than you of these poor charms that you desire... and that your burning hands are already exploring with such ardour? Can you not see, by the fire that is setting me ablaze, that I am just as impatient as you to experience the pleasure which you are telling me of? Ah! Take me, enjoy me, my tender brother, my best friend! Make your Eugénie your victim: sacrificed at your beloved hands she will always be victorious."

The ardent Franval – who, as one might have expected, had put on this charade of delicacy only to be a more effective seducer – soon took advantage of his daughter's credulity, and once all the obstacles had been cleared from his path, both by the principles with which he had nurtured her impressionable soul, and by the art with which he captivated her at this supreme moment, he completed his wicked conquest, and became himself, with complete impunity, the destroyer of a virginity which Nature and his own position had committed to his safe keeping.

Several days were spent in a state of mutual rapture. Eugénie, old enough to experience the pleasures of love, and encouraged by his philosophizing, indulged herself in it with frenzy. Franval taught her all love's mysteries, and showed her all its paths; the more he multiplied his acts of homage, the more he chained his captive to him: she would have liked to receive him in a thousand temples at once; she accused her friend's imagination of not being adventurous enough: it seemed to her that he was concealing something from her. She complained of her youth, and of an innocence that perhaps did not make her seductive enough, and if she desired to be better instructed, it was so that no means of inflaming her lover's desire could remain unknown to her.

They returned to Paris, but the criminal pleasures which this perverted man had rapturously enjoyed had so delectably stimulated his physical and moral faculties that the inconstancy which usually led him to break off his affairs failed to break the bonds of this one. He fell passionately in love, and from this dangerous passion there inevitably ensued the most cruel abandonment of his wife... What a victim, alas! Mme de Franval, aged thirty-one at the time, was in the flower of her beauty; an impression of sadness, inevitable given the sorrows that were consuming her, made her even more intriguing; drowned in tears, in her dejection and melancholy... her beautiful hair falling in disarray on a breast of alabaster... her lips amorously pressed to the cherished portrait of her faithless and tyrannical spouse, she resembled those lovely virgins painted by Michelangelo in the depths of their sorrow. But she was still unaware of what would soon complete her torment. The way Eugénie was being educated; the essential things that were being kept from her, or which were mentioned only to inspire her hatred of them; the fact that she was certain her daughter would never be allowed to exercise those duties that Franval despised; the short time she was allowed to see the girl; her fear that the singular education she was receiving would sooner or later bring crime in its wake; and last but not least the follies of Franval: his daily harshness towards her, when she was intent only on anticipating his every wish and all her charms were deployed only in arousing his interest or giving him pleasure – these were, so far, the sole causes of her affliction. By what darts of pain would this tender and sensitive soul not be pierced as soon as she discovered the whole truth!

Meanwhile, Eugénie's education continued. She herself had desired to retain her tutors until she was sixteen, and her talents, her wide learning, the graces which were each day developing in her, all bound Franval more closely to her: it was easy to see that he had never loved anyone as he loved Eugénie.

Only one aspect in the initial arrangements made for Mlle de Franval's life had been altered: the time of the lectures. Those sessions alone with her father became much more frequent, and lasted late into the night. Only Eugénie's governess was aware of the full extent of the affair, and she could be counted on sufficiently for there to be no fear of her indiscretion. There were also a few changes in Eugénie's meals: she now ate with her parents. This circumstance, in a house like that of Franval's, soon made it possible for Eugénie to get to know other people, and to be desired by them as a potential wife; her hand was asked for by several persons. Franval, assured of his daughter's heart, thought he had absolutely nothing to fear from these approaches; he had not sufficiently reflected that the flood of proposals might end up giving everything away.

In a conversation with her daughter, a favour ardently desired by Mme de Franval, and one that she obtained all too rarely, this loving mother informed Eugénie that M. de Colunce wanted her hand in marriage.

"You know this man, my daughter," said Mme de Franval. "He loves you, he is young and likeable; he will be rich, he is merely waiting for your consent... nothing more than your consent, my daughter... What answer shall I give him?"

Eugénie, taken by surprise, blushed, and replied that she still felt little inclination for marriage, but that her father could be consulted: she would have no other wishes than his.

Mme de Franval, seeing nothing untoward in this reply, bided her time for a few days, and when she eventually found an opportunity to mention it to her husband, she communicated to him the intentions of young Colunce's family, and those which Colunce himself had expressed; she added her daughter's answer. It can easily be imagined that Franval already knew everything, but, disguising his real emotions, though without keeping them entirely under control, he said drily to his wife:

"Madam, I must emphatically ask you not to get involved with Eugénie's affairs: from the care I took to keep her away from you, it ought to have been easy for you to recognize how much I desired that everything concerning her should be absolutely none of your business. I repeat my orders on this subject... You will not forget them again, I presume?"

"But how am I to answer Colunce, Monsieur, since I am the one who is being asked?"

"You will say that I am touched by the honour shown me, but that my daughter was born with certain defects which are obstacles to the bonds of marriage."

"But, monsieur, these defects are not real: why do you want me to dissemble, and why should you deprive your only daughter of the happiness she may find in marriage?"

"Have those bonds made you particularly happy, madam?"

"Not all women have the failings that I must have had, given that I have not succeeded in tying you to me," she said, and added, with a sigh, "or else not all husbands are like you."

"Wives... false, jealous, domineering, flirtatious or devout... husbands, wicked, inconstant, cruel or despotic: that in a nutshell is how all individuals on earth are, madam; do not expect to find any paragon of virtue."

"And yet everyone gets married."

"Yes, the stupid or the lazy; you never marry, says one philosopher, *unless you do not know what you are doing, or no longer know what to do with your life.*"

"So we should let the human race die out?"

"We might as well: a plant that produces nothing but poison cannot be pulled up too soon."

"Eugénie will not thank you for this excess of severity towards her."

"Does this marriage appear to please her?"

"Your wish is her command, she has said."

"Well, madam, my wish is that you should drop this marriage forthwith."

And M. de Franval left: once more forbidding his wife in the strictest terms ever to mention the topic again.

Mme de Franval did not fail to report to her mother the conversation she had just had with her husband, and Mme de Farneille, more astute and better acquainted with the effects of the passions than her charming daughter, immediately suspected that there was something supernatural at work here.

Eugénie saw little of her grandmother – for an hour at most, on social occasions, and always under the eyes of Franval. Mme de Farneille, desirous of shedding light on this business, therefore asked her son-in-law to send her granddaughter to see her, and to allow her to stay a whole afternoon, so as to distract her from an attack of migraine she was suffering from. Franval conveyed an acerbic reply, to the effect that there was nothing Eugénie feared so much as the vapours; that he would nonetheless take her to where her presence was requested; but that she would not be able to stay long, because she was under an obligation to return for her course in physical science, which she was assiduous in attending.

They went to Mme de Farneille's; she did not hide from her son-in-law her astonishment at his refusal to accept the proposed marriage.

"You can, I think," she continued, "permit without any anxiety your daughter to convince me of the defect which, according to you, must deprive her of marriage?"

"Whether this defect is real or not, madam," said Franval, a little surprised at his mother-in-law's resoluteness, "the fact is that it would cost me dear to marry off my daughter, and I am still too young to consent to such sacrifices; when she is twenty-five she can act as she sees fit: she must not count on my acceptance until that time."

"And are you of the same sentiments, Eugénie?" said Mme de Farneille.

"There is one way in which they are different, madam," said Mlle de Franval with considerable firmness. "Monsieur says he will allow me to marry at twenty-five, but I protest to you and to him, madam, that I will never, my whole life long, take advantage of such a permission... which, to my way of thinking, would merely contribute to the unhappiness of my existence."

"Nobody has a 'way of thinking' at your age, mademoiselle," said Mme de Farneille. "There is something extraordinary in all this which I am going to have to unravel."

"I really hope you will, madam," said Franval, leading his daughter away. "You will even do well to employ your clergy to solve the riddle, and when all the powers at your disposal have done the best they can, and when you have finally discovered the truth, then will be the time for you to tell me whether I am wrong or whether I am right to oppose Eugénie's marriage."

The sarcasm generally levelled at the ecclesiastical advisors of Franval's mother-in-law was also aimed at one worthy person in particular, whom it is relevant to introduce at this moment, since the sequence of events will soon show him in action.

This was the spiritual director of Mme de Farneille and her daughter... one of the most virtuous men in the whole of France, honest, charitable, a man of great sincerity and prudence: M. de Clervil, untouched by any of the vices so often attached to his priestly office, had only amiable and useful qualities. A reliable supporter of the poor, a sincere friend of those who lived in the lap of luxury, ready with consolation for the wretched – this worthy man had all the gifts which make a man likeable, and all the virtues that make a sensitive man.

When he was consulted, Clervil answered with his usual common sense that before taking any decision on this business, the reasons M. de Franval might have for opposing his daughter's marriage should be prised out, and although Mme de Farneille let fall a few remarks that might have aroused suspicions about the all-too-real affair, the cautious spiritual director rejected these ideas and, finding them much too deeply insulting for Mme de Franval and her husband, he repudiated them indignantly.

"Crime is such a painful thing, madam," this worthy man would sometimes say, "it is so implausible to suppose that any person of sense would voluntarily transgress all the boundaries of modesty and override all the constraints of virtue. It is only ever with the most extreme repugnance that I can bring myself to attribute such misdeeds to anyone. We should incline but rarely to suspect anyone of vice; our suspicions are often the work of our own self-love, almost always the product of a tacit comparison that we make in the depths of our hearts: we rush into imputing evil to others, so as to have the right to consider ourselves better. If we ponder it sufficiently, would it not be better, madam, that a secret crime was never revealed, rather than to imagine illusory crimes by an unpardonably over-hasty judgement, and thus needlessly to sully, in our eyes, people who have never committed any faults other than those which our pride has attributed to them? And indeed, is it not in every way advantageous if we work on this principle? Is it not immeasurably less necessary to punish a crime than essential that this crime be prevented from spreading? By leaving it in the shadows which it seeks, is it not, as it were, reduced to nothing? Once it is made public knowledge, scandal is bound to ensue, and the account one gives of it arouses the passions of those who are inclined to the same kind of misdeed; the blindness inseparable from crime increases the hopes nursed by the guilty man that he will be luckier than the man who has just been brought to justice: it is not a lesson he has been given, it is a piece of advice, and he yields to excesses that he would perhaps never have dared commit, were it not for the indiscreet fuss and bother – falsely considered to be justice – which is, in fact, misconceived severity, or vanity in disguise."

The only decision taken in this first discussion was that of verifying the exact reasons why Franval was so reluctant to allow his daughter to be married, and those for which Eugénie shared this same way of thinking. It was resolved not to embark on any plan of action until these reasons had been laid bare.

"Well, Eugénie!" said Franval, that evening, to his daughter. "As you can see, they are trying to separate us: are they going to succeed, my child?... Will they manage to break the sweetest ties of my entire life?"

"Never... never! Have no fear, my dearest friend! These bonds which you delight in are just as precious to me as to you; you have not deceived me, you have made clear to me, as you tied those bonds, the extent to which they shocked our customs and manners and, unafraid to transgress usages which, as they vary from climate to climate, can have nothing sacred about them, I deliberately accepted those bonds, I wove them without remorse: so you need not fear that I will break them."

"Alas! Who knows?... Colunce is younger than I am... He has all that is needed to charm you. Do not pay any heed, Eugénie, to a residual confusion that is no doubt blinding you. Maturity, and the light of reason, will make the prestige evaporate, and soon produce regret. You will pour it out into my heart, and I will never forgive myself for having been a cause of it!"

"No," replied Eugénie firmly, "no, I have decided that I will never love anyone but you; I would consider myself the most unhappy of women if I had to take a husband... I!" she continued heatedly. "I – join my destiny to that of a stranger who, not having as you do a twofold reason to love me, would at best measure his feelings by his desires!... Abandoned, despised by him, what will become of me afterwards? Will I be a prude, a bigot or a whore? Ah, no! No! I prefer to be your mistress, my dear. Yes, I love you a hundred times more than the prospect of being reduced to play in the world one or other of those revolting roles... But what is the cause of all these manoeuvres?" continued Eugénie with bitterness... "Do you know, my dear, what it is?... Your wife... she alone... her implacable jealousy... Have no doubt about it, those are the sole reasons for the disasters with which we are threatened... Ah! I cannot blame her: everything is simple... everything is easy to understand... everything is possible when it is a matter of keeping you. What would I not do, if I were in her place, and someone were trying to steal your heart from me?"

Franval, strangely moved, embraced his daughter a thousand times, and she, more encouraged by these criminal
caresses, and giving her heinous soul even greater scope
and energy, ventured to tell her father, with unforgivable
shamelessness, that the only way for the two of them to
escape observation was to give her mother a lover. This
plan amused Franval, but being much more wicked than
his daughter, and wishing to prepare her young heart by
imperceptible degrees for all the impressions of hatred
against his wife which he wanted to sow there, he replied
that such a vengeance seemed too mild to him, that there
were many other ways of making a wife unhappy when she
was a source of annoyance to her husband.

In this way, several weeks passed, during which Franval
and his daughter finally decided on the first plan to bring
this monster's virtuous wife to despair, believing, correctly,
that before resorting to even more unworthy stratagems, they
should at least try that of finding a lover – a stratagem which
would not only lay the basis for further developments, but if
it succeeded, would then inevitably force Mme de Franval to
stop busying herself with the faults of others, since she would
have obviously committed several of her own. To carry out
his plan, Franval cast his eyes over all the young men of his
acquaintance, and after pondering the matter deeply, he found
only Valmont who seemed capable of serving his designs.

Valmont was thirty, had a handsome face, intelligence, a
good deal of imagination, not the slightest principle and,

consequently, was just the man to perform the role proposed. Franval invited him to dinner, and taking him aside as they left the table, said:

"My friend, I have always considered you worthy of me; now is the time to prove that I was not wrong. I am asking for a proof of your feelings... but a quite extraordinary proof."

"What do you have in mind? Explain yourself, my friend, and never doubt how eager I am to be of use to you!"

"What do you think of my wife?"

"Delightful, and if you were not her husband, I would have been her lover long ago."

"That consideration shows great delicacy, Valmont, but it does not mean a thing to me."

"What?"

"I am going to surprise you... It is precisely because you love me... precisely because I am the husband of Mme de Franval that I am insisting you become her lover."

"Are you mad?"

"No, but I am whimsical... and capricious – as you're aware, having known me for a long time... I want to bring virtue to grief, and I am sure it is you who will ensnare it."

"What a crazy idea!"

"Not a word: it is a masterpiece of reasonableness."

"What! You want me to—"

"Yes, I want it, I demand it of you, and I will no longer regard you as my friend if you refuse me this favour... I will serve you... I will procure for you such moments... I will grant you them in abundance... you will reap the benefit of them, and as soon as I am quite certain of my destiny, I will throw myself, if necessary, at your feet, to thank you for being so obliging."

"Franval, I am not your dupe. There is something bizarre in all this... I am not going to do anything until I know everything."

"Yes... but I think you are displaying too many scruples; I suspect that you are still not strong-minded enough to understand the plans I have afoot... Still a few prejudices... a touch of chivalry, I'll be bound?... You will tremble like a child when I tell you everything, and will no longer be ready to act."

"I, tremble?... I am indeed quite taken aback by your opinion of me: you must know, my dear fellow, that there is no misdeed in the world... no, not a single one, however irregular it may be, capable of alarming my heart for a single instant."

"Valmont, have you sometimes cast your eyes on Eugénie?"

"Your daughter?"

"Or my mistress, if you prefer."

"Ah, you rogue! Now I understand."

"This is the first time in my life I have found you quick on the uptake."

"So – word of honour, you are in love with your daughter?"

"Yes, my friend, just like Lot; I have always been imbued with such a great respect for the holy scriptures, and so

convinced that we could win heaven by emulating its heroes!...
Ah, my friend, the madness of Pygmalion no longer sur-
prises me...Is not the whole world full of these moments of
weakness? Were they not necessary in the beginning so as to
populate the earth? And something that was not an evil then
can surely not have become one since? What a crazy idea! A
pretty woman is not allowed to tempt me, simply because I
made the mistake of bringing her into the world? That which
is supposed to unite me even more intimately to her turns out
to be a reason for keeping her away from me? Because she
resembles me, because she is my own flesh and blood, because
she in other words unites in her person all the reasons which
can act as the basis for the most ardent love, am I supposed to
look on her coldly?... Ah, what sophistry!... What absurdity!
Let us leave those ridiculous constraints to idiots: they are not
made for souls such as ours. The power of beauty and the
holy rites of love are untouched by trivial human conventions,
which they destroy by their ascendancy, just as the rays of the
sun in broad daylight purify the bosom of the earth from the
fogs which cover it at night. Let us trample underfoot those
dreadful prejudices which are always inimical to happiness:
if they sometimes seduced the reason, it was only ever at the
price of the most intense pleasures... Let them always be held
in contempt by us!"

"You have convinced me," replied Valmont, "and I am all
too willing to grant that your Eugénie must be a delightful mistress: she is an even more striking beauty than her

mother, and if she does not altogether possess, as your wife does, that languor which overcomes the soul so voluptuously, she has that sparkle which quite conquers us, and which seems, in a word, to subjugate all resistance we try to put in its path; if the one woman seems yielding, the other is more of a challenge; what the one permits, the other offers, and I can well imagine that the latter has more charm."

"But it is not Eugénie I am giving you, it is her mother."

"Ah! And what is the reason for that?"

"My wife is jealous, she bothers me, she keeps me under surveillance; she wants to marry off Eugénie: I have to get her to commit some misdeeds in order that I can successfully conceal my own. So you must have her... disport yourself with her, for a while... then betray her... and I must catch you in her arms... punish her, or else by means of this discovery purchase peace on both sides, given our mutual errors... But no love, Valmont: keep a cool head. Trap her, and do not allow her to get the upper hand; once feelings come into it, my plans can all go to the Devil."

"Have no fear: she would be the first woman really to inspire me with any warmth of feeling."

So our two rogues agreed on their arrangements, and it was resolved that, in very few days' time, Valmont would make an attempt on Mme de Franval with full permission to employ whatever he might need to succeed... even including an avowal of Franval's affair, as the most powerful means to persuade that honest woman to take revenge.

Eugénie, to whom the plan was confided, was vastly amused by it; the heinous creature dared to say that if Valmont succeeded, it would be necessary, so as to ensure that her own happiness was as complete as it could possibly be, for her to ascertain with her own eyes her mother's downfall – and see that heroine of virtue yielding, beyond any shadow of a doubt, to the attractions of a pleasure which she so sternly condemned.

Finally the day arrived on which the most upright and unfortunate of women was not only to receive the most painful blow that could be inflicted on her, but on which she was also to be so insulted by her husband as to be abandoned… handed over by him to the man he was happy to see himself dishonoured by… What madness!… What contempt for all principles! Whatever can be the reason for which nature is capable of creating hearts as depraved as theirs?…

A few preliminary conversations had prepared the scene; Valmont, indeed, was a close enough friend of Franval for his wife, who had already found herself in such a situation quite without risk, to imagine no danger in remaining alone with him. All three were in the drawing room; Franval rose.

"I must be off," he said. "I have an important piece of business waiting for me… It is as good as leaving you with your governess, madam," he added with a laugh, "to leave you with Valmont: he is so well behaved… But if he forgets his manners, tell me, I do not love him so much that I am prepared to surrender my rights to him…"

And the impudent rascal sped away.

After a few unexceptional remarks, occasioned by Franval's joke, Valmont said that he found his friend quite changed these last six months.

"I was not bold enough to ask him the reason," he continued, "but there seems to be something causing him anxiety."

"What is certain," replied Mme de Franval, "is that he is a cause of the most dreadful anxiety to others."

"Heavens above! What is this I hear?... Could it be that my friend has given you cause for offence?"

"If only that were all we had to worry about!"

"Please be so good as to tell me; you know my eagerness to serve you... my inviolable attachment to you."

"A series of horrible and eccentric actions... corrupt moral standards and, indeed, every kind of misdeed... Can you believe it? We are being offered for his daughter the most advantageous marriage... he won't have it..."

And at this point, the cunning Valmont averted his eyes, with the air of a man who has grasped what is happening... groans at it... and is afraid to explain his thoughts.

"Monsieur!" continued Mme de Franval. "What I am telling you comes as no surprise? Your silence is most strange."

"Ah, madam! Is it not better to hold one's tongue than to talk when it means plunging the person one loves into despair?"

"What is this riddle? Explain it, I beg you."

"How can you expect me not to tremble at the prospect of opening your eyes?" said Valmont, seizing with warmth one of the hands of this charming woman.

"Oh, monsieur!" resumed Mme de Franval with the greatest agitation. "Either say not a word more, or explain yourself in full, I insist… The situation in which you are keeping me is appalling."

"Perhaps much less so than the state to which you yourself reduce me," said Valmont, letting his gaze, burning with ardent love, fall on the woman he was seeking to seduce.

"But what is the meaning of all this, monsieur? You begin by alarming me, you make me yearn for an explanation; having the boldness to intimate to me things which I must not and cannot allow, you deprive me of the means of learning from you the cause of such cruel worry. Speak, monsieur, speak, or you will reduce me to despair."

"Very well, I will be less obscure, since you insist, madam, and although it costs me a considerable effort to rend your heart… you shall learn the cruel reason that lies behind the way your husband has turned down M. de Colunce… Eugénie…"

"Well?"

"Well, madam, Franval adores her. Less her father at present than her lover, he would prefer to be forced to renounce the light of day rather than give up Eugénie."

Mme de Franval had not been able to hear this fateful disclosure without her head spinning so much that she lost control of her senses. Valmont made haste to bring her round, and as soon as he had succeeded, he continued:

"You see, madam, how difficult it is to learn what you have just forced me to tell you... I would for anything in the world..."

"Leave me, monsieur, leave me," said Mme de Franval, in a state that can barely be described. "After such a violent shock, I need to be alone for a moment."

"And you would let me leave you in this situation? Ah! Your pain is too intensely felt by my soul for me not to ask for permission to share it; I have inflicted the wound: allow me to heal it."

"Franval in love with his daughter! Just Heavens! That creature whom I bore in my womb, she it is who is tearing it so cruelly apart!... A crime so dreadful... Ah, monsieur, is it possible?... Are you sure?"

"If I still had room for doubt, madam, I would have kept quiet; I would have preferred a hundred times not to say anything to you rather than alarm you for nothing. It is from your husband himself that I have learnt for sure of this infamy: he confided it to me. Whatever the situation, a little calm, I beg you; let us now think of the means to break up this affair, rather than removing our doubts about it, and those means lie within you alone..."

"Ah! Make haste to tell me what they are!... This crime fills me with horror."

"A husband with the character of Franval, madam, cannot be won back by virtue. Your husband sets little store by the good behaviour of women: it is merely, he claims, the product of their pride or their temperament, and all that they do to keep themselves in our good books is done much more to make them feel pleased with themselves than to satisfy us or bind us to them... Pardon me, madam, but I will not disguise the fact that I think much the same as him on this subject: I have never seen a woman succeeding in destroying her husband's vices by virtuous means. Behaviour more or less the same as Franval's would pique him much more intensely, and would bring him back to you much more effectively; jealousy would be the inevitable consequence: and how many hearts have been brought back to love by that ever-infallible means! Your husband, when he sees that the virtue he is used to in you, and which he makes so bold as to hold in contempt, is much more the product of mature reflection than of a careless indifference or lack of desire, will really learn to appreciate it in you, once he thinks that you are capable of failing in virtue... He imagines... he makes so bold as to say that if you have never had any lovers, it is because none have ever made an attempt on you: prove to him that it depends on you alone whether this happens... to avenge yourself on his misdeeds and his contempt for you. Perhaps you will have committed a small evil, by the light of your strict principles, but how many evils you will have forestalled! What a husband you will have converted! And for a trivial slight to the goddess you revere, what a follower of her cult will you not have brought back to her temple? Ah, madam! Let me merely appeal to your reason. Through the conduct I am making so bold as to prescribe for you, you are bringing Franval back for good, you are making him your eternal captive: he will fly from you if you adopt the opposite course, and never return. Yes, madam, I can assure you: either you do not love your husband, or you must not waver."

Mme de Franval, quite taken aback by these words, remained speechless for a while. When she finally managed to reply, remembering the way Valmont had looked at her and his first words to her, she cunningly said:

"Monsieur, supposing that I were to yield to the advice you are giving me, who do you think I should cast my eyes on so as to cause the greater anxiety to my husband?"

"Ah!" exclaimed Valmont, not seeing the trap she was laying for him. "My dear, divine friend... on the man who loves you best in the whole world, on the man who has adored you ever since he has known you, and who swears at your feet to die at your orders..."

"Get out, monsieur! Get out!" Mme de Franval interrupted imperiously. "And never show yourself before my eyes again! Your plot is discovered; you are imputing to my husband these misdeeds – of which he is quite incapable – so as to further your treacherous attempts at seduction. Let me tell you that even if he were guilty, the means you are proposing to me would be too repellent to my heart for me to employ them for an instant. Never do a husband's transgressions justify those of a wife: they must constitute additional reasons for her to behave well, so that the just man, whom the Eternal God finds in the afflicted cities that are about to suffer the effects of his wrath, may if possible avert from them the flames that are soon to devour them."

With these words, Mme de Franval left and, asking for Valmont's servants, she obliged him to withdraw... quite shamefaced at his first attempts.

Although this charming woman had seen through the ruses of Franval's friend, what he had said coincided so closely with her fears and those of her mother that she resolved to do all in her power to convince herself of these cruel truths. She went to see Mme de Farneille, told her what had happened, and came home, determined to carry out the plan that we are about to see her set in motion.

It has long been said, and quite rightly, that we have no greater enemies than our own valets: always jealous, always envious, it seems that they seek to lighten their chains by bringing out the faults in us which set us below them and thus for a short while allow their vanity to enjoy a dominance over us that Fate in reality denies them.

Mme de Franval had one of Eugénie's servant girls bribed: she was assured of a pension, an agreeable future and the outward appearance of doing a good deed; all this swayed this creature's mind, and she undertook, the following night, to put Mme de Franval in a position where she could no longer doubt her misfortune.

The crucial moment arrived. The unfortunate mother was brought into a small room next to the apartment where her treacherous husband offended each night against the laws of matrimony and the laws of heaven. Eugénie was with her father; several candles were alight on a corner table, illuminating the crime... The altar was prepared, the victim placed herself on it, the sacrificer followed her... Mme de Franval was left only with her despair, her enraged love and her courage... She broke down the doors holding her back, threw herself into the apartment and there, falling to her knees and weeping at the feet of that incestuous father, she exclaimed to Franval:

"Oh, you who are making my life a misery! You, to whom I have done nothing that merits such treatment... You whom I still adore, whatever insults my love exposes me to, see my tears... and do not reject me! I beg you to take mercy on this unhappy woman who, deceived by her own weakness and your seduction, thinks she can find happiness in the midst of shamelessness and crime... Eugénie, Eugénie, are you trying to plunge a dagger into the womb which gave you birth? Cease forthwith to make yourself a partner in a crime whose horror is concealed from you!... Come... run to me... see my arms ready to receive you! See your unhappy mother, at your knees, begging you not to offend against both honour and nature!... But if you both refuse my pleas," continued the despairing woman, putting a dagger to her heart, "this is how I am going to escape the foul stains with which you seek to cover me: I will spatter you with my blood, and it is only over my wretched body that you will be able to consummate your crimes."

That the hardened soul of Franval could resist this spectacle will come as no surprise to those who are beginning to be familiar with the villain, but that Eugénie's soul refused to yield is quite inconceivable.

"Madam," said the corrupt girl, with the most cruel indifference, "I must confess that I cannot see how your reason can approve the ridiculous scene that you have come to make in your husband's apartment. Is he not master of his own actions? And when he finds my actions acceptable, do you have any right at all to criticize them? Do we bring up your escapades with M. de Valmont? Do we disturb you in the midst of your pleasures? Have the decency to respect ours, or do not be surprised if I am the first to press your husband to take steps that will force you to do so…"

At this moment Mme de Franval suddenly lost patience; the full force of her wrath turned against the unworthy creature who could so forget herself as to speak to her like this, and, rising in a fury, she flung herself on her… But the hateful, cruel Franval, seizing his wife by her hair, furiously dragged her away from his daughter and out of the room, and throwing her violently down the stairs, he sent her hurtling in a faint, covered in blood, against the door of one of her women servants who, awoken by this horrible noise, made haste to pull her mistress away from the wild anger of her tyrant, who had already come running after to finish off his wretched victim...

She was led to her own apartment, the door was locked behind her, she was taken care of, and the monster who had just treated her with such wild rage flew back to his detestable companion to spend the night as tranquilly as if he had not lowered himself beneath the level of the fiercest beasts through such execrable crimes, so deliberately humiliating for her... so horrible, in a word, that we blush at the necessity which we are under to reveal them.

The unhappy Madame de Franval could no longer take refuge in her illusions; not a single one remained for her to indulge in; it was all too clear that the heart of her husband – the most precious thing in her whole life – had been stolen from her... And by whom? By the girl who owed her the most respect... and who had just spoken to her with such insolence! She had also suspected that the whole stratagem set up by Valmont was merely a hateful trap to tempt her into guilty actions – if possible – and if not, to attribute similar actions to her in such great number that they would outweigh and justify those, a thousand times more serious, that they had dared to commit against her.

Nothing could be more certain. Franval, informed of Valmont's lack of success, had instructed him to replace truth with imposture and indiscretion... and to make it public knowledge that he was Mme de Franval's lover. It had been decided by this little group that they would counterfeit some abominable letters which would make clear, in the most unequivocal manner, the existence of the liaison to which this unhappy wife had nonetheless refused to be a partner.

Meanwhile, in a state of despair, and indeed wounded in several parts of her body, Mme de Franval fell seriously ill, and her barbaric husband, refusing to see her, and not even condescending to enquire how she was, set off with Eugénie for the country, on the pretext that as fever was abroad in his house, he did not want to expose his daughter to it.

Valmont presented himself several times at Mme de Franval's door during her illness, but without being granted admittance even once. Closeted with her tender mother and M. de Clervil, she saw absolutely nobody; consoled by such dear friends, so well placed to exert an influence on her, and restored to life by their care, after forty days she was in a fit state to see people again. Then Franval brought his daughter back to Paris, and thorough preparations were made with Valmont to ensure that he was equipped with weapons capable of countering those which, it seemed, Mme de Franval and her friends were about to deploy against them.

Our villain appeared in his wife's apartment as soon as he thought she was in a fit state to receive him.

"Madam," he said to her coldly, "you must not doubt the extent to which I have taken your state of health into consideration; it is impossible for me to disguise from you that

44

this alone is responsible for the restraint shown by Eugénie: she was determined to lay the most serious charges against you, concerning the way you treated her. However convinced she may be of the respect a daughter owes her mother, she cannot, however, ignore the fact that this mother puts herself in the worst possible position imaginable when she throws herself on her daughter, a dagger in her hand: an act of such rash impetuosity, madam, could, if it opened the eyes of the government to your conduct, inevitably lead to your honour and liberty being one day put at risk."

"I was not expecting such recriminations, monsieur," replied Mme de Franval, "and when, having been seduced by you, my daughter makes herself at once guilty of incest, adultery, libertinage and of the most hateful ingratitude towards the mother who gave birth to her... yes, I have to confess, I did not imagine that, after this complex tangle of horrors, it would be for me to fear any complaints: you must need all your art, all your wickedness, monsieur, for you to excuse crime with such audacity and level an accusation against innocence."

"I am perfectly aware, madam, that the pretext for your scene was the hateful suspicions that you have the temerity to nurse against me, but imaginary grievances do not justify crimes: what you have imagined is false, but what you have done is unfortunately only too real. You show surprise at the reproaches my daughter uttered against you on the subject of your affair with Valmont, but, madam, she is revealing

the irregularities of your behaviour only after the whole of
Paris has already done so: this situation is so well known…
and the proof, unfortunately, so indubitable, that those who
mention it in your presence are at most committing an act
of imprudence, but not of slander."

"I, monsieur!" said that worthy wife, rising indignantly
to her feet… "I am supposed to be having an affair with
Valmont?… Just Heavens! And you dare to say such a thing!"
And, in floods of tears, she added: "You ungrateful man! Such
is the reward for my affection… such is the recompense for
having loved you so much: you are not content with insulting me so cruelly, it is not enough for you to seduce my own
daughter, you have to go further and boldly justify your own
crimes by imputing to me others which would be more dreadful for me than death itself…" She pulled herself together.
"So you have proof of this affair, you say, monsieur? Show it;
I demand that it be made public; I will force you to broadcast
it to the whole world, if you refuse to show it to me."

"No, madam, I will not show it to the whole world; it is
not ordinarily a husband who makes the open disclosure of
such things: he bewails them, and hides them as well as he
can, but if you demand it, madam, I will certainly not refuse
it to you…" And, taking a wallet from his pocket, he said:
"Sit down, this must be verified calmly; a tantrum, or any
display of emotion, would have a negative effect and would
quite fail to convince me. So recover your composure, I beg
you, and let us discuss this with a cool head."

Mme de Franval, perfectly convinced of her innocence, had no idea what to think of these preparatory remarks, and her surprise, mixed with panic, kept her in a state of violent suspense.

"Here, to begin with, madam," said Franval, as he emptied one of the pockets of the wallet, "is your entire correspondence with Valmont for the last six months or so: do not accuse that young man of imprudence or indiscretion; he is doubtless too honest to dare to be so lacking in regard for you. But one of his servants, more artful than Valmont is attentive, managed to procure this precious evidence of your exemplary behaviour and your eminent virtue." He leafed through the letters that he had scattered over the table, and continued: "I hope you will not mind if, from amongst all this commonplace chatter of a woman who has been inflamed... by a perfectly likeable man... I choose one which struck me as even more lively in expression and decisive than the others... Here it is, madam:

My nuisance of a husband is dining this evening in his little house in the suburbs with that horrible creature... to whom I cannot possibly have given birth: come, my dear, and console me for all the sorrows that those two monsters are inflicting on me... But what am I saying? Is it not the greatest service they could render me at present, and will not their affair prevent my husband from noticing ours? Let him tie the knot as tightly as he pleases, but he

47

should at least not take it into his head to break the knot
which ties me to the only man I have ever truly adored
in all the world.

"Well! Madam?"

"Well! Monsieur, I wonder at you," replied Mme de Franval. "Every day adds to the incredible esteem that you should deserve, and whatever great qualities I had recognized in you up until now, I must confess that I did not know that you could also boast those of a forger and slanderer."

"Ah! So you deny it?"

"Not at all: all I ask is for convincing proof; we will have judges appointed – experts, and we will ask, if you agree, for the severest punishment to be meted out to whichever of us two is the guilty party."

"What a case of brazen effrontery! But come, I prefer that to pain... Let us proceed. That you have a lover, madam," said Franval, shaking the other pocket of the wallet, "with a handsome face, and a *nuisance of a husband*, nothing, assuredly, could be simpler, but that at your age you should be keeping that lover, and at my expense, is something that you will permit me to find rather less straightforward... However, here is a promissory note for a hundred thousand écus, either paid by you, or signed by you personally in favour of Valmont; just look over it, I beg you," added that monster, holding it before her eyes without allowing her to touch it:

48

To Zaide, jeweller.
The present note guarantees the payment of the sum
of twenty-two thousand livres to the account of M. de
Valmont, as duly arranged with him.

(Signed)
Farneille de Franval

"*To Jamet, horse-seller, six thousand livres...* That was for the pair of bay horses which is currently Valmont's pride and joy, and admired throughout Paris... Yes, madam, here is a bill for *three hundred thousand two hundred and ninety-three livres and ten sols*, of which you owe more than a third, and the rest of which you have most scrupulously paid off... Well madam?"

"Ah, monsieur, as for this fraud, it is too gross to cause me the slightest disquiet. I will demand merely one thing to confound those who are concocting such inventions against me: that the people for whom I have, it is said, signed these notes, appear, and swear on oath that I did indeed have business with them."

"They will do so, madam, have no doubt: would they themselves have warned me of your behaviour if they had not been determined to maintain the truth of their declarations? Were it not for me, one of them was going to have had you summoned today..."

Bitter tears sprang from the lovely eyes of that unhappy woman; her courage could no longer sustain her, and she was overwhelmed by despair, punctuated by the most alarming symptoms: she beat her head against the marble pillars around her, and pummelled her own face.

"Monsieur," she cried, flinging herself at the feet of her husband, "have the goodness to get rid of me, I beg you, by less slow and terrible means! Since my existence is an obstacle to your crimes, destroy it at a single blow... do not push me so slowly into my grave... Am I guilty because I loved you?... Because I rebelled against a situation that was so cruelly stealing your heart away from me?... Very well! Punish me for it, barbarian! Yes, take this weapon," she said, throwing herself on her husband's sword, "take it, I tell you, and pitilessly pierce my breast, but let me at least die worthy of your esteem, let me take with me to the grave, as my sole consolation, the certainty that you think me incapable of the infamies of which you accuse me only in order to conceal your own..."

She was on her knees, bent double at Franval's feet, her hands bleeding and wounded by the naked point of the weapon she was trying to wrest from him in order to thrust it into her breast. Her lovely breast was bare, her hair fell across it in disorder, drenched by the tears that were pouring from her eyes: never did pain appear more poignant and more expressive, never had it been seen in a guise so touching, so alluring and so noble.

"No, madam," said Franval, resisting her moves, "no, it is not your death that we desire, but your punishment. I well understand your repentance, and your tears do not surprise me: you are furious at being discovered; these dispositions in you please me, they allow me to presage an amendment in your life… which no doubt will more rapidly bring about the fate I am preparing for you, and I will hasten away to give it my attention."

"Stop, Franval!" exclaimed the unhappy woman. "Do not spread word of your dishonour, do not tell the public that you are simultaneously a perjurer, a forger, an incestuous father and a slanderer… You want me out of the way, I will fly from you, I will go and seek some place of safety where I will forget the very memory of you… you will be free, you will be criminal with impunity… Yes, I will forget you… if I can, cruel man, or if your lacerating image cannot be wiped away from my heart, if it continues to pursue me in my deepest darkness… I will not destroy it, faithless man, that effort would be more than I could manage – no, I will not destroy it, but I will punish myself for my blindness, and I will bury henceforth, in the horror of the tomb, the guilty altar on which you were too dearly cherished…"

At these words, the last fervent outbursts of a soul overwhelmed by recent illness, the unfortunate woman swooned and fell unconscious. The cold shades of death spread across the rosy complexion of that beautiful face, already ravaged by the sting of despair; only a lifeless mass could still be seen, although grace, modesty and decency – all the allure of virtue – could not altogether abandon it. The monster left: he went off to enjoy, with his criminal daughter, the dreadful triumph that vice, or rather wickedness, is bold enough to celebrate over innocence and affliction.

These details gave the greatest pleasure to Franval's execrable daughter: she would have liked to see everything herself... If only the horror could have been taken even further, if only Valmont could have triumphed over her mother's stern resistance, if only Franval could have caught them in the act. What means – if all this had taken place – what means of justification would have remained to their victim? And was it not important to deny her any such means? Such was Eugénie.

Meanwhile, Franval's unhappy wife, having only her mother's welcoming breast on which to shed her tears, did not long hold back the new cause of her grief. It was then that Mme de Farneille imagined that M. de Clervil's age and profession, and the personal consideration in which he was held, could perhaps produce some good effects on her son-in-law: nothing is more trusting than misfortune. She informed the worthy ecclesiastic, as best she could, of the wild behaviour of Franval; she convinced him of the truth of everything he had never been willing to believe, she enjoined him above all not to use on such a villain anything other than that persuasive eloquence which acts more on the heart than on the mind. She recommended that once he had spoken to that faithless man, he should obtain an interview with Eugénie, in which he would likewise deploy all the means he felt most likely to point out to that unfortunate girl the abyss yawning at her feet, and to bring her back, if possible, to her mother's arms and the ways of virtue.

Franval, informed that Clervil was asking to see his daughter and himself, had time to hatch a plot with her and, once their plans had been laid, they let Mme de Farneille's spiritual director know that they were both ready to hear him. The credulous Mme de Franval placed all her hopes on the eloquence of this spiritual guide: the afflicted seize so avidly on imaginary straws and, to procure for themselves a happiness which truth denies them, they turn their illusions, with the greatest artistry, into reality!

Clervil arrived; it was nine o'clock in the morning; Franval received him in the apartment where he habitually spent the nights with his daughter; he had had it decorated with all imaginable elegance, while at the same time allowing one to see a certain disorder which indicated his criminal pleasures... Eugénie, in hiding nearby, could hear everything, so she would be better prepared for the interview that had been arranged for her in turn.

"It is only with the greatest anxiety that I might seem importunate, monsieur," said Clervil, "that I make so bold as to present myself before you. People in my profession are commonly such a burden to people who, like you, spend their time in the pleasures of this world, that I reproach myself for having consented to the desires of Mme de Farneille and asked for permission to talk with you for a few moments."

"Take a seat, monsieur, and so long as the language of justice and reason holds sway in your words, you need never fear that you will cause me annoyance."

"You are adored by a young wife full of charm and virtue, whom you are accused of making very unhappy, monsieur: she has nothing on her side except her innocence and her candour, and only her mother able to lend an ear to her lamentations, and yet she still idolizes you in spite of your wrongdoing – you can easily imagine the horror of the position she is in!"

"I would be glad, monsieur, if we could get straight to the facts; it seems to me that you are beating around the bush. What is the purpose of your mission to me?"

"To bring you back to happiness, if such a thing were possible."

"And so, if I find myself happy as I am, you cannot have anything further to say to me?"

"It is impossible, monsieur, for happiness to be found in crime."

"I quite agree, but the man who, by profound study and mature reflection has managed to train his mind to find not a hint of evil in anything, to view with the most tranquil indifference all human actions, to consider them all as the necessary results of a power, whatever it may be, sometimes good and sometimes perverse, but always imperious, which inspires us sometimes to commit actions which men approve and sometimes actions which they condemn, but never anything which upsets or disturbs that power itself – that man, I say, as you will agree, monsieur, can find himself just as happy, behaving the same way as I do, as you are in the career which you are pursuing. Happiness is ideal, it is the product of imagination; it is a way of being moved, which depends only on our way of seeing and feeling; there is, apart from the satisfaction of their needs, nothing which makes all men equally happy; each day we see an individual made happy by exactly the same thing which is a cause of the greatest displeasure to another: thus no happiness is certain, and there can exist for us no other happiness than that which we form on the basis of our bodily constitution and our principles."

"I know, monsieur, but if the mind deceives us, our conscience never leads us astray: it is the book in which Nature writes all our obligations."

"And do we not deal with that factitious conscience exactly as we please? Habit can bend it; it is for us a piece of soft wax which can assume any shape under our fingers; if this book were as sure a guide as you say, would not man have a conscience that never varied? From one end of the earth to another, would not all actions be the same for him? But is that actually the case? Does a Hottentot tremble at what frightens a Frenchman? And does a Frenchman not do every day things that would incur punishment in Japan? No, monsieur, no, there is nothing real in the world, nothing which merits praise or blame, nothing worthy of being rewarded or punished, nothing which, though it is unjust here, is not legitimate five hundred leagues away – no real evil, in a word, and no constant good."

"Do not believe it, monsieur: virtue is no imaginary chimera; it is not a matter of knowing whether a thing is good here, or bad a few geographical degrees away, for us to assign to it a precise quotient of crime or virtue, and to be assured of finding happiness in the choice we have made: man's sole felicity can be found only in his most entire submission to the laws of his country; he must either respect them, or be wretched; to transgress them is immediately to run the risk of unhappiness. It is not, if you like, from these actions in themselves that stem the evils which assail us, when we indulge in them even though they have been forbidden to us: it is from the injury that these actions, intrinsically good or bad, inflict on the social conventions of the climate we inhabit. There is certainly nothing wrong in preferring to take a stroll along the boulevards rather than walking down the Champs-Elysées: nonetheless, if a law were to be promulgated forbidding the citizens to walk down the boulevards, the man who infringed that law would perhaps draw on himself an eternal chain of disasters, even though he had done nothing out of the way by infringing it. Furthermore, the habit of overriding ordinary constraints soon leads us to break more serious ones and, from error to error, we end up committing crimes which are properly punished in every country in the whole world, and properly inspire dread in all reasonable creatures which inhabit the globe, under whichever pole it might be. If there is not a universal conscience for mankind, there is thus a national conscience, relative to the existence we have received from Nature, onto which her hand imprints our duties, in marks which we cannot erase without endangering ourselves. For example, monsieur, your family is accusing you of incest; whatever sophistries one may have used to justify this crime and lessen its horror, whatever specious arguments have been deployed on this topic, whatever authority one has fallen back on by citing examples from neighbouring countries, it is nonetheless clearly demonstrated that this crime, which is a crime only among certain peoples, is nevertheless dangerous wherever the laws forbid it. It is no less certain that it can draw in its wake the most dreadful consequences, as well as crimes that are the inevitable consequence of this first transgression... crimes, I say, which are most properly viewed with horror by men. If you had married your daughter on the banks of the Ganges, where these marriages are permitted, perhaps you would have committed a quite unimportant misdeed: but in a government where such relations are prohibited, by offering this revolting spectacle to the public – and to the eyes of a wife who adores you, and who this betrayal is bringing to the grave – you are, there is no doubt about it, committing a terrible action, a crime which tends to break the holiest bonds in nature, those which, connecting your daughter to the person who gave her birth, should make that person the most worthy of her respect and the most sacred thing in her world. You are forcing this girl to despise these precious duties; you are making her hate the woman who bore her in her womb; you are preparing, without realizing it, weapons which she may turn against you; you are presenting her with no system of thought, and inculcating in her no principle which does not carry your condemnation written upon it, and if her hand should one day strike at your life, you yourself will have sharpened the blade."

"Your way of reasoning, so different from that of people in your profession," replied Franval, "persuades me first of all to confide in you, monsieur. I could deny your charge: my frankness in disclosing myself to you will oblige you, I hope, to believe equally in the misdeeds of my wife, when I employ the same truth to reveal them to you that will guide the confession of my own misdeeds. Yes, monsieur, I love my daughter, I love her passionately, she is my mistress, my wife, my sister, my confidante, my friend, my sole god on earth – she has in short all the titles which can win the homage of a heart, and all the homage of my heart is due to her. These feelings will last as long as my life; so I must, doubtless, justify them, since I cannot possibly renounce them.

"The first duty of a father towards his daughter is indisputably, as you will agree, monsieur, that of procuring for her the greatest sum of happiness possible: if he has not succeeded in that, he has failed his daughter; if he has succeeded, he is immune from all reproach. I neither seduced nor forced Eugénie: this is a highly significant fact, do not forget it; I did not hide the world from her, I showed her at length the roses of marriage as well as the thorns that are found in it. Then I offered myself; I left Eugénie free to choose, she had plenty of time to think it over, she did not hesitate, she protested that she could find happiness with no one but me: was I wrong to give her, for her happiness, something which, in full knowledge of the facts, she appeared to prefer to everything else?"

"These sophistries do not justify anything, monsieur; you should not have put it into your daughter's head that the person whom it was impossible for her to love without committing a crime could become the object of her happiness: however beautiful the external appearance of a fruit, would you not repent of offering it to someone if you were sure that death were hidden in its flesh? No, monsieur, no, the only person whose advantage you sought, in this wretched behaviour, was yourself, and you have made your daughter both accomplice and victim in it; this conduct is unforgivable... And that virtuous and sensitive wife, whose heart you take pleasure in breaking – what wrong has she committed in your eyes? What wrong, you unjust man... apart from the wrong of idolizing you?"

"That is what I was hoping you would say, monsieur, and it is on this subject that I expect your full trust in me; I have some right to hope for it, no doubt, after the completely frank and open way in which you have just seen me agreeing with the accusations levelled against me!"

Whereupon Franval, showing Clervil the false letters and promissory notes that he claimed had been written by his wife, stated firmly that nothing was more real than all this evidence, or Mme de Franval's affair with the man it referred to.

Clervil knew everything.

"Well!" he said firmly to Franval. "Was I right to tell you that an error, at first seen as inconsequential in itself, can, by habituating us to transgress boundaries, lead to the most extreme forms of crime and evil-doing? You began by an action that was insignificant in your eyes, and you can now see all the infamies you are forced to commit so as to justify or conceal it… Will you take my advice, monsieur? Let us throw all these unforgivable black slanders on the fire, and rid ourselves, I beg you, of the least memory of them."

"This evidence is real, monsieur."

"It is fake."

"You cannot be sure of that: are your surmises enough to prove that I am wrong?"

"Allow me, monsieur: the only evidence I have that it is real is your word, and it is greatly in your interest to support your accusation; for me to consider this evidence fake, I have as evidence the testimony of your wife, in whose interest it would equally be to tell me that it was real – if it *were* real. This is how I reach my conclusion, monsieur… People's self-interest is the vehicle of all their stratagems, the great driving force of all their actions; wherever I encounter it, the torch of truth is immediately lit for me: this rule has never deceived me, I have been applying it for forty years, and besides, will your wife's virtue not set at nought this abominable slander in the eyes of everyone? Is it with her honesty, is it with her candour, is it with the ardent love she still bears you, that anyone would permit themselves such atrocious deeds? No, monsieur, no, these are not the first steps of crime: since you know its effects so well, you should have been better at pulling the strings that lead to it."

"Insults, monsieur!"

"Forgive me: injustice, slander and libertinage revolt my soul to such a degree that sometimes I am not able to master the agitation into which these horrors plunge me. Let us burn these papers, monsieur, I must insist once again... Let us burn them, for your honour and for your peace of mind."

"I never imagined, monsieur," said Franval, rising to his feet, "that with the ministry you perform, it was so easy to become the apologist for – indeed the protector of – misconduct and adultery. My wife is sullying my name, she is ruining me, I can prove it to you: your blindness to her real character makes you prefer to accuse me myself and to suppose rather that I am a slanderer than that she is a treacherous, debauched woman! Well, monsieur, the laws will decide; all the law courts in France will resound to the echo of my complaints: I will take my proofs to them, I will make my dishonour public knowledge in them, and then we will see if you have the good nature, or rather the stupidity, to protect such a shameless creature against me."

"I will withdraw then, monsieur," said Clervil, also rising. "I did not imagine that your warped mind could also infect the qualities of your heart and that, blinded by an unjust vengeance, you could become capable of maintaining in cold blood what a moment of madness had engendered... Ah! Monsieur, all this convinces me more thoroughly than ever that when man has transgressed the most sacred of his duties, he soon permits himself to break all the others... If on reflection you come back to your senses, have the goodness to tell me, monsieur, and you will always find, in your family and in me, friends ready to receive you... May I be permitted to see mademoiselle your daughter, for a moment?"

"You are perfectly free to do so, monsieur; when you see her, I would exhort you to put forward more eloquent arguments, or less specious reasons, when presenting her with those luminous truths, in which I, unfortunately, have only detected blindness and sophistry."

Clervil went to Eugénie's apartment. She was waiting for him in the most coquettish and elegant *déshabillé*; this sort of indecency, the product of self-abandon, corruption and crime, was shamelessly evident in her gestures and her looks, and the treacherous woman, insulting the graces which made her beautiful in spite of herself, combined all that can inflame vice with all that revolts virtue.

Since it does not behove a girl to enter into such profound detail as it does a philosopher like Franval, Eugénie restricted herself to making taunting remarks; little by little, she moved to the most decided flirtation, but as she soon realized that such attempts at seduction were a waste of time, and that a man as virtuous as the one with whom she was dealing would not fall into her trap, she swiftly cut the knots that held the flimsy clothes concealing her charms and, striking a pose of the greatest disarray before Clervil had time to realize what she was up to, she started to scream:

"Wretched man! Take this monster away! Let his crime be at least hidden from my father. Just Heavens! I expect pious advice from him... and the dishonest man makes an attempt on my virtue!... Look," she said to her servants as they came running at the sound of her cries, "look at the state the shameless man has put me in. That is what they are like, those oh-so-kindly worshippers of a divinity they insult – scandal, debauchery, seduction – these are the components of their morality, and deceived by their false virtue, we are foolish enough to go on revering them!"

Clervil, deeply angered by the scene, managed nonetheless to conceal his discomfiture, and coolly withdrawing through the crowd, he said tranquilly:

"May Heaven preserve this unfortunate woman... may it make her mend her ways if it can, and may no one in her house ever raise a hand against feelings of virtue... which I came much less to sully than to rekindle in her heart!"

This was the only reward that Mme de Farneille and her daughter were able to reap from an interview on which they had based so many hopes. They were far from knowing the degradation which crime causes in the soul of villains: remonstrances that would be effective on other people are merely provocative when employed against them, and it is in the very lessons given by virtue that they are spurred on to do evil.

From this time on, things became more rancorous on both sides: Franval and Eugénie clearly saw that they would have to convince Mme de Franval of her alleged wrongs in such a way that it would no longer be possible for her to doubt them further, and Mme de Farneille, working in concert with her daughter, was quite seriously proposing to have Eugénie abducted. The plan was discussed with Clervil; that honest friend refused to take part in such extreme projects: he had, he said, been too badly treated in this whole business to do anything other than implore mercy for the guilty – he earnestly requested it, and was constant in his refusal to perform any other office or mediation. What sublime sentiments! Why is such nobility so rare in men of the cloth? Or, why was this man's office so sullied?

Let us begin by relating the stratagems of Franval.

Valmont reappeared.

"You are a complete fool," the criminal lover of Eugénie told him, "you are quite unworthy to be my pupil, and I will trumpet your name abroad through the whole of Parisian society if, in a second interview, you do not succeed better

with my wife. You must have her, my friend, really and truly
– my eyes must prove to me that she has been vanquished…
I must be allowed to take away from that hateful creature
every means of excuse and defence."

"But what if she resists?" replied Valmont.

"You will use violence… I will make sure there is no one
around… Frighten her, threaten her: what does it matter?…
I will regard as so many signal services rendered on your
part all the means you use to gain your victory."

"Listen," Valmont then said, "I agree to your proposal, I
give you my word that your wife will yield, but I demand one
condition, and the deal is off if you refuse. Jealousy must
play absolutely no part in our arrangements, as you know:
so I demand that you let me spend just a quarter of an hour
with Eugénie… You cannot imagine what I will do when I
have enjoyed the pleasure of your daughter's company for
a few moments…"

"But Valmont…"

"I can understand your fears, but if you believe me to
be your friend, I cannot forgive them: all I aspire to is the
pleasure of seeing Eugénie alone and conversing with her
for a moment."

"Valmont," said Franval, in some astonishment, "you
are putting far too high a price on your services: I know, as
well as you, all the absurdities of jealousy, but I idolize the
woman of whom you are speaking, and I would rather give
up my fortune than her favours."

"I am not after them, you can rest assured."

And Franval, who knew well that, among all his acquaintances, no person was capable of serving him like Valmont, and was anxious not to let him slip from his grasp, said with some ill humour:

"Well! I will say it again: your service does not come cheap; if you carry it out through these means, you can consider any debt of gratitude on my part paid."

"Oh! Gratitude is only ever the price of honest service; your heart will never feel any gratitude for the service I am about to render you: more than that, it will cause us to fall out within two months... Come, come, my friend, I know what man is like... his shortcomings... his strayings and all the consequences they entail: place this animal, the most wicked of all, in any situation you like, and I will not fail to predict a single consequence that will follow from the initial premise. So I want to be paid in advance, or else I will not do a thing."

"I accept," said Franval.

"Well then!" replied Valmont. "Everything depends now on your wishes: I will act whenever you want."

"I need a few days to make my preparations," said Franval, "but in four days at the most I will be yours."

M. de Franval had brought up his daughter in such a way that he could be sure it would not be an excess of modesty that would lead her to refuse to fit in with the plans he had laid with his friend, but he was jealous, as Eugénie well knew; she adored him at least as much as she was cherished by him, and she confessed to Franval, as soon as she knew what was afoot, that she greatly feared this private interview might have consequences. Franval, who thought he knew Valmont well enough to be sure that there would be intellectual entertainment but no emotional entanglements, allayed his daughter's fears as well as he could, and the preparations were made.

It was just at this moment that Franval learnt, through reliable servants entirely loyal to him in his mother-in-law's house, that Eugénie was in grave danger and that Mme de Farneille was on the point of obtaining an order to have her taken away. Franval had no doubt that the plot was Clervil's work and, putting Valmont's plans to one side for the time being, he concentrated wholly on getting rid of the wretched ecclesiastic whom he so wrongly believed to be the instigator of the whole business. He distributed gold: that powerful vehicle of every vice was placed by him in a thousand different hands. Finally, six trusty rascals promised to carry out his orders.

One evening when Clervil, who often had dinner at Mme de Farneille's, was leaving alone and on foot, he was surrounded and seized... and told that his arrest was at the behest of the government. He was shown a counterfeit order, thrown into a post-chaise, and conveyed in all haste to the dungeons of an isolated chateau belonging to Franval, in the depths of the Ardennes. There, the unfortunate priest was handed over to the caretaker of the property like a wicked man who had made an attempt on the life of his master, and the most elaborate precautions were taken to ensure that this wretched victim, whose sole failing had been to show too much indulgence towards those who had so cruelly mistreated him, would never again show his face to the light of day.

Mme de Farneille was plunged into despair. She had no doubt but that the deed was the work of her son-in-law. The need to find Clervil slowed down somewhat the plans for Eugénie's abduction: with a very limited set of acquaintances and little real credit, it was difficult to pursue simultaneously two such important objectives; besides, this daring act on Franval's part had created quite an impression. So their one thought was that of saving the priest, but all their searches were in vain: our villain had taken such careful measures that it was quite impossible to discover a thing. Mme de Franval did not dare to question her husband too closely: they had still not spoken to each other since the last scene, but when much is at stake, any hesitation is reduced to nought; she finally worked up the courage to ask her tyrant if his plan was to add to all the woes he had inflicted on her the further crime of depriving her mother of the best friend she had in the whole world. The monster defended himself; his mendacity went so far as to offer his own services in the search; and seeing that, in order to prepare for the scene with Valmont, he needed to calm her mind, he repeated his offer to do his utmost to ensure that Clervil would be found, lavished caresses on his credulous wife, and assured her that whatever infidelity he had committed, it was becoming impossible for him not to adore her from the bottom of his heart. Mme de Franval, indulgent and sweet-natured as ever, and always happy when anything brought her closer to a man who was dearer to her than her own life, went along with all the desires of that treacherous husband, anticipated them, served them and shared them without exception, not daring to make the most of the moment, as she should have done, to persuade that barbarian to treat her better, and not plunge his unhappy wife every day into an abyss of pain and suffering. But even if she had done so, would her attempts have been crowned with success? Could Franval, so false in all life's actions, be any more sincere in one whose only attraction, in his opinion, lay in the fact that it involved overstepping several limits? He would doubtless have promised anything for the mere pleasure of breaking all bounds; perhaps he would even have liked her to ask him to swear on oath so he could add the attractions of perjury to his horrible pleasures.

Franval, in a state of perfect tranquillity, had no other thought than that of troubling the tranquillity of those around him: such was the nature of his character – vindic-tive, turbulent and impetuous whenever he was given cause for disquiet, bent on recovering his peace of mind at what-ever price and, with this aim, clumsily employing the very means that were most likely to ensure that he lost it once more. If he recovered his peace of mind, he used all his moral and physical faculties solely to cause harm to others: in this way, always in a state of agitation, he either had to forestall the stratagems that he constrained others to employ against him, or employ similar stratagems against them.

Everything had been arranged to satisfy Valmont, and his private interview lasted more than an hour in Eugénie's own apartment.

There, in a decorated room, Eugénie, naked on a pedestal, represented a young savage woman tired out after the hunt, leaning on a palm trunk, whose elevated branches concealed numberless lights disposed in such a way that their reflection, falling entirely on the charms of this beautiful girl, heightened them in the most artistic way imaginable. The little theatre in which this living statue made her appearance was surrounded by a moat, six feet wide, which served the young savage as a barrier and prevented her from being approached from any side. At the edge of the moat was placed Valmont's chair, and tied to the chair was a silk cord: by manipulating this cord, he made the pedestal rotate in such a way that the object of his worship could be viewed from every angle, while she was posing in such a way that, however the arrangement was disposed, she was always delightful to look at. Franval, hidden behind a decorative shrubbery, could simultaneously keep both his mistress and his friend under observation, and as they had last agreed, the examination was to last for half an hour... Valmont took his place... He was intoxicated: never, he said, had so many alluring prospects presented themselves to his sight; he yielded to the ardent transport overwhelming him. The cord, its length varying ceaselessly, offered him new prospects at every moment: to which would he sacrifice? Which did he prefer? He did not know; everything in Eugénie was so beautiful! But the minutes went by; they go by quickly in circumstances such as these; the hour struck: the chevalier lost control of himself, and incense flew to the feet of the god whose sanctuary was forbidden him. A gauze curtain fell: it was time to withdraw.

"Well, are you satisfied?" said Franval, going to join his friend.

"She is a delightful creature," replied Valmont, "but Franval, a word of advice: do not take such a risk with any other man, and be thankful for the feelings that, in my heart, must guarantee you are safe from all dangers."

"I am counting on it," replied Franval, quite seriously. "So now you must take action at the earliest opportunity."

"I will prepare your wife tomorrow... as you can imagine, we will need a preliminary conversation... In four days' time, you can be sure of me."

They exchanged their pledges and went their separate ways. But it was hardly to be expected that, after such an encounter, Valmont should feel like betraying Mme de Franval, or granting his friend a conquest of which he had become all too envious. Eugénie had made on him such a profound impression that he could not give her up: he was resolved to obtain her as his wife, at whatever price. When he thought it over at more leisure, once he had overcome the disgust aroused in him by Eugénie's affair with her father, he was quite convinced that, as his fortune was the equal of Colunce's, he could with equal justice lay claim to the same marriage. So he imagined that if he presented himself as a husband, he could not be refused, and if he acted with boldness to break Eugénie's incestuous relationship, and promised her family that he would succeed in doing so, he would infallibly win the object of his worship... even if he had to deal with Franval, whom he hoped by dint of his own courage and skill to overcome.

Twenty-four hours were sufficient to mull over these reflections, and it was with his head full of ideas of this kind that Valmont made his way to Mme de Franval's. She was expecting him; in her last conversation with her husband, it will be remembered that she had almost made it up with him, or rather that, having yielded to the insidious stratagems of that treacherous man, she could no longer refuse to see Valmont. She had, nonetheless, raised the problem of the letters, the words and the ideas expressed by Franval, but he, seemingly unconcerned by any of this, had given her his full assurance that the surest way of making people think that all these things were false, or no longer an issue, was to see his friend in the usual way: to refuse, he insisted, would justify his suspicions; the best proof that a woman can give of her fidelity, he had told her, is to continue to see publicly the man with whom the gossips say she is having an affair. This was all sophistry, and Mme de Franval was only too aware of it, but she hoped for an explanation from Valmont; the desire to obtain one, coupled with the desire not to anger her husband, had caused her to turn a blind eye to everything that should reasonably have prevented her from seeing the young man in question. He arrived, and Franval, making haste to leave, left them together as he had on the previous occasion. The explanations could have been animated and lengthy, but Valmont, intent on his plans, cut the preliminaries short, and came straight to the facts.

"Oh! Madam! Do not look upon me any longer as that same man who showed himself guilty before you the last time we spoke!" he hastened to say. "At that time, I was in league with the wicked plans of your husband, today I am here to make reparation, but trust me, madam; take to heart, I beg you, the word of honour I give you that I have not come here either to lie to you, or to mislead you in any way."

Then he admitted the story of the false notes and the counterfeit letters; he apologized a thousand times over for having gone along with the plot; he warned Mme de Franval of the new horrors that were still being demanded of him and, to emphasize his sincerity, he confessed his feelings for Eugénie, disclosed what had happened, promised to break off with Franval and abduct Eugénie from him, then take her to Picardy, to one of the properties owned by Mme de Farneille, if both these ladies would grant him their permission and promise him, as a reward, the woman he would thus have rescued from the abyss.

Valmont's words, and his frank confession, were so imbued with the character of truth that Mme de Franval could not fail to be convinced. Valmont was an excellent match for her daughter: after Eugénie's misbehaviour, could she hope for anything better? Valmont was taking responsibility for everything; there was no other way of putting a stop to the dreadful crime which was the despair of Mme de Franval. Could she not flatter herself, moreover, that her husband would again feel affectionate towards her, once the only affair which could really become dangerous for herself and him had been broken off? These considerations proved decisive: she yielded, but on condition that Valmont gave her his word he would not fight with her husband, would leave the country after handing over Eugénie to Mme de Farneille, and would remain there until Franval had calmed down sufficiently for him to be consoled for the loss of his illicit love, and finally consent to the marriage. Valmont promised to fulfil all these demands; Mme de Franval, for her part, agreed to answer for her mother's intentions: she assured him that she would not place a single obstacle in the path of the resolutions they had made together; and Valmont withdrew, repeating his apologies to Mme de Franval for having participated in her dishonest husband's schemes against her.

The following day, Mme de Farneille, having been informed of all this, left for Picardy, and Franval, plunged into the perpetual whirlpool of his pleasures, counting on Valmont's firm support, and no longer worried about Clervil, fell headlong into the trap laid for him, with the same naivety that he so often wished to see in others, when in his turn he wanted to ensnare them.

For about six months, Eugénie, who was approaching her seventeenth year, had frequently been going out alone, or with a few of her female companions. On the eve of the day when Valmont, as arranged with his friend, was to make an attempt on Mme de Franval, she happened to be quite alone watching a new play at the Théâtre des Français; she was coming home from there with the intention of going to join her father in a house where he had arranged to meet her, so they could then go together to the house where they habitually dined… Hardly had Mlle de Franval's coach left the Faubourg Saint-Germain, when ten masked men stopped the horses, opened the carriage door, seized hold of Eugénie and threw her into a post-chaise next to Valmont, who, taking every precaution to stifle her cries, ordered the greatest haste, and was outside Paris in the twinkling of an eye.

It had unfortunately proved impossible to get rid of Eugénie's servants and carriage, and so Franval was quickly alerted to what had happened. Valmont, to cover his tracks, had counted on Franval's uncertainty as to the road he would take, and on the two or three hours' head start he would

75

inevitably have. All that was needed was for him to reach the property belonging to Mme de Farneille, where there were two women he could count on, and a post-chaise waiting to take Eugénie to the frontier: a place of safety unknown even to Valmont, who would immediately cross over into Holland and return only to marry his mistress, as soon as Mme de Farneille and her daughter had informed him that there were no obstacles remaining. But fortune allowed these carefully laid plans to founder on the horrible designs of the villain concerned.

Franval, once apprised of what had happened, did not lose an instant: he rushed to the posting station and asked for which roads horses had been hired, from six o'clock in the evening onwards. At seven, a Berlin coach had left for Lyon, and at eight a post-chaise for Picardy: Franval did not hesitate – the Berlin for Lyon could assuredly not be what he was looking for, but a post-chaise heading for a province where Mme de Farneille owned land – that was what he was after: it would be madness to doubt it. So he quickly had the eight best post-horses put to the carriage he was in, he ordered his servants to take small horses, he bought and loaded pistols while they were harnessing the horses and he flew like an arrow in the direction indicated by love, despair and vengeance. Changing horses at Senlis, he learnt that the post-chaise he was pursuing had only just left... Franval ordered them to ride like the wind; to his misfortune, he caught up with the carriage: his servants and he,

pistol in hand, stopped Valmont's postilion, and the impetuous Franval, recognizing his adversary, blew out his brains
before he could defend himself, dragged away the swooning
Eugénie, threw himself with her into his carriage and was
back in Paris before ten in the morning. Hardly concerned
by all that had just occurred, Franval's only thoughts were
for Eugénie... Had the treacherous Valmont attempted to
take advantage of the circumstances? Was Eugénie still
faithful, and her criminal liaison unsullied? Mlle de Franval
reassured her father: Valmont had merely outlined his plan
to her and, filled with the hope of marrying her soon, he
had refrained from profaning the altar on which he wished
to plight his pure troth.

Eugénie's asseverations reassured Franval... But his wife...
was she a party to these manoeuvres... had she given her
assistance? Eugénie, who had had the time to find out, certi-
fied that this was all her mother's work; she poured the most
hateful names upon her; and she insisted that the fateful
conversation in which Franval had imagined that Valmont
was prepared to serve him so well was the one in which he
had betrayed him most shamelessly.

"Ah!" said Franval, in a fury. "Why does he not have a
thousand lives?... I would tear them all from him, one after
the other!... And my wife!... Just when I was seeking to
deceive her... she was the first to trick me... that creature
who everyone thinks is so sweet and gentle... that angel of
virtue!... Ah, treacherous, treacherous woman, you will pay

77

dearly for your crime!... My vengeance will have blood, and I will draw it, if needs be, with my own lips from your faithless veins... Calm yourself, Eugénie," continued Franval, in his violent rage... "yes, calm yourself, you need peace and quiet, go and rest for a few hours, I will see to all this by myself."

Meanwhile Mme de Farneille, who had set spies along the road, was soon alerted to all that had happened. Once she knew that her granddaughter had been recaptured and Valmont killed, she hastened to Paris... Filled with fury, she gathered her council around her there and then; they made it clear to her that the murder of Valmont would deliver Franval into her hands; the credit which hitherto he had enjoyed and she had feared would immediately vanish, and thereupon she would become mistress both of her daughter and of Eugénie; but they recommended that she take steps to prevent a scandal and, for fear of proceedings that might sully her name, request an order that would safeguard her son-in-law. Franval, immediately apprised of this advice and of the actions that would ensue, learning simultaneously that his affair was public knowledge, and that his mother-in-law was only waiting – so they said – for disaster to strike him so that she could take advantage of it, hurried straight away to Versailles, saw the minister, told him everything, and received for all reply the advice to go quickly and take refuge in the land he possessed in Alsace, on the Swiss border. Franval immediately returned home and, intent on not failing in his vengeance, on punishing his wife's treachery and on making sure he was still in possession of persons who were sufficiently dear to Mme de Farneille that she would not, at least not publicly, risk taking sides against him, he resolved to leave for Valmor, the property the minister had advised he go to, only if he were accompanied by his wife and his daughter... But would Mme de Franval accept? Filled with guilt for her treachery which had been the cause of all that had happened, would she be able to leave for such a distant place? Would she dare to entrust herself without fear to the arms of an outraged husband? This is what was worrying Franval: to discover the lie of the land, he immediately went to see his wife, who already knew everything.

"Madam," he said to her calmly, "you have plunged me into an abyss of misfortune by your over-hasty indiscretions; while I can only criticize the effect, I nonetheless applaud the reason – which assuredly lay in the love you bear for your daughter and myself, and since the first misdeeds were my doing, I must forget those that ensued. My dear and tender better half," he continued, falling at his wife's knees, "will you accept a reconciliation that nothing will ever affect again? That is what I am offering you, and here is the means of sealing it..."

Thereupon he laid at his wife's feet all the counterfeit documents of Valmont's supposed correspondence.

"Burn it all, my dear, I beg you," continued the traitor, with feigned tears, "and forgive what jealousy made me do: let us banish all bitterness from between us. I have many failings, I own as much, but who knows if Valmont, to further his plans, did not blacken my character to you much more than I deserve?... If he had dared to say that I could ever stop loving you... that you could ever be anything other than the most precious thing, and the most worthy of my respect, in the whole world – Ah! Dear angel! If he had sullied himself with such slanders, how right I would have been to rid the world of such a cheating rogue and such an impostor!"

"Oh, Monsieur!" said Mme de Franval in tears. "Is it possible to conceive the atrocities that you have committed against me? What trust do you think I can place in you, after such horrors?"

"I want you still to love me, O most tender and most loveable of women! I want you to be convinced, as you lay the blame for my many errors on my head alone, that this heart of mine, over which you have always and ever reigned, could never have been capable of betraying you... Yes, I want you to know that there is not a single one of my errors which has not brought me even closer to you... The further I found myself from my dear wife, the less I could see any possibility of finding her in anything I did; no pleasures or feelings could match those which she gave me and which my inconstancy had forced me to lose, and even in the arms of her image I was longing for the reality... O dear and divine friend! Where can I ever find a soul like yours? Where can I enjoy the favours that can be gathered in your arms? Yes, I abjure all the error of my ways… Now I wish to live for you alone in all the world… to re-establish, in your embittered heart, that love so justly destroyed by any misdeeds… of which I wish to forget the very remembrance."

It was impossible for Mme de Franval to resist such tender expressions coming from a man she still adored: is it possible to hate him whom one has loved? Is it possible, for a delicate and sensitive soul of the kind this charming woman had, to see in cold blood, at your feet, in a flood of remorseful tears, the person who was once so precious? Sobs escaped from her breast and, pressing to her heart her husband's hands, she said:

"I, who have never stopped idolizing you, you cruel man! I am the one you take pleasure in reducing to despair!… Ah! Heaven is my witness that of all the afflictions you could visit on me, the fear of having lost your love, or of being the object of your suspicions, was the most heart-rending of all!… And what weapon do you still use to outrage me?… My daughter!… It is with her hands that you are piercing my heart… you want to force me to hate her whom Nature has made so dear to me!"

"Ah!" said Franval with even greater ardour. "I want to bring her to kneel at your feet, and I want her to abjure, as I have done, both her shamelessness and her misdeeds… may she, as I have, obtain pardon. Let the three of us concentrate on nothing more than our mutual happiness. I will return your daughter to you… return my wife to me… and let us flee."

"Flee? Great God!"

"My adventure is creating a stir... I could be ruined tomorrow... My friends, the minister, all of them have advised me to travel to Valmor... Will you be kind enough to follow me, my dear? Could it be that, at the very moment I am asking you at your feet to forgive me, you would break my heart with a refusal?"

"How you alarm me... What! This whole business..."

"Is being treated as a murder, and not as a duel."

"Oh God! And I am the reason for it!... Tell me what to do... tell me what to do, I am at your disposal, dear husband... I will follow you, if needs be, to the ends of the earth... Ah! I am the most wretched of women!"

"Say the most fortunate, rather, since every instant of my life is going to be devoted to changing into flowers the thorns I strewed at your feet... Is not a desert enough when two people love each other? Furthermore, this situation cannot last for ever: my friends are informed and will take action."

"And what about my mother?... I would like to see her..."

"Ah! Do not think of it, my dearest, I have sure and certain proof that she is turning Valmont's relatives against me... and that she herself has sided with them to seek my downfall..."

"She is not capable of such a thing: stop imagining these incredible horrors; her soul is made for love and has never stooped to imposture... You never really appreciated her, Franval... Why could you not love her as I did? In her arms we would have found happiness on earth! She was an angel of peace, offered by heaven for the errors of your life: your injustice spurned her heart, which was always open to cherish you, and, through thoughtlessness or capriciousness, through ingratitude or libertinage, you deliberately deprived yourself of the best and most tender friend that Nature had created for you!... And so I am not to see her again?"

"No, I must insist that you do not... the moments are so precious! You can write to her, you can describe my repentance... Perhaps she will yield when she hears of my remorse... perhaps one day I will regain her esteem and her heart; everything will quieten down, we will return... we will return to enjoy, in her arms, her pardon and her affection... But right now we must be off, my dearest... we must, this very hour, and the carriages are already waiting for us..."

Mme de Franval, frightened, did not dare reply; she gathered her thoughts: was not Franval's wish her command? The traitor flew to his daughter; he led her to the feet of her mother; the false creature threw herself down just as deceitfully as her father; she wept, she implored her mercy, she obtained it. Mme de Franval embraced her: it is so difficult to forget that you are a mother! However much your children have insulted and injured you... the voice of Nature is so imperious in a sensitive soul that a single tear from those sacred persons is enough to make us forget in them twenty years of faults or failings.

They left for Valmor. The extreme haste they were obliged to make on this journey seemed sufficient explanation, in the eyes of Mme de Franval, still credulous and blind as she was, for the small number of domestic servants they were taking with them. Crime avoids all eyes... and fears them: as its security is possible only in the shadows of mystery, it wraps itself within them when it wishes to act.

Once they were in the country, deeds matched words: assiduous concern, close attention, respect, every proof of affection on the one side... and every proof of the most violent love on the other, all were lavished in seductive profusion on the unfortunate Mme de Franval... At the ends of the earth, far from her mother, in the depths of a terrible solitude, she found herself happy, because she had, she said, her husband's heart, and because her daughter, unceasingly at her knees, was intent only on pleasing her.

The apartments of Eugénie and her father were no longer next door to each other: Franval was lodged at the far end of the chateau, Eugénie right next to her mother; and decency, good order, modesty, replaced at Valmor, in the highest possible degree, the irregular life they had led in the capital. Every night, Franval went to his wife, and the cheating rogue, enfolded in the very bosom of innocence, candour and love, had the shameless audacity to foster her hope with his horrors. He was so cruel that he was not appeased by those naive and fervent caresses which the most delicate of women showered on him, and it was from the torch of love itself that the villain lit the torch of vengeance.

It is easy to imagine, however, that Franval's assiduities for Eugénie showed no sign of slackening. Each morning, while her mother was dressing, Eugénie would meet her father in a distant corner of the gardens; she would obtain from him in her turn both the advice necessary for the conduct of the moment and the favours she was far from willing to surrender totally to her rival.

They had not been in this secluded spot a week, when Franval learnt that Valmont's family was hot on his heels, and that the whole matter was going to be treated in the most serious fashion. It was becoming impossible, people said, to pass it off as a duel, as there had unfortunately been too many witnesses. Furthermore, they told Franval that nothing was more certain than that Mme de Farneille was at the head of her son-in-law's enemies, intent on ruining him by depriving him of his liberty, or forcing him to leave France, so as to bring back under her wing without further ado the two cherished persons who had left her.

Franval showed his wife these letters: she immediately took up her pen to calm her mother, to persuade her to consider things in a different frame of mind and to depict the happiness she herself had been enjoying ever since misfortune had softened the soul of her unfortunate husband; she assured her further that any means set in motion to get her to return to Paris with her daughter would be in vain, that she was resolved not to leave Valmor until her husband's business had been settled, and that if the malice of his enemies, or the absurd sentence of his judges, made him endure an arrest that would sully his name, she was quite determined to follow him into exile.

Franval thanked his wife, but, having no desire to await the fate which was being prepared for him, he warned her that he was going to spend some time in Switzerland, that he was leaving Eugénie with her, and that he begged both of them not to leave Valmor until his destiny had been settled; whatever this destiny might be, he would in any case return to spend twenty-four hours with his dear wife to discuss together the means of returning to Paris, if nothing prevented them, or if it did, to go and live in safety somewhere else.

Having made these resolutions, Franval, who had not lost sight of the fact that the imprudence of his wife with Valmont was the sole cause of his setbacks, and whose every thought breathed vengeance, communicated to his daughter that he was waiting for her at the far end of the estate and, having shut himself away with her in a solitary summer house, made her swear the blindest obedience to all he was going to command her to do, and then embraced her, and spoke to her in these terms:

"You are losing me, my daughter... perhaps for ever..."

And, seeing Eugénie in tears, he told her:

"Calm yourself, my angel, it depends on you whether our happiness can be revived, and whether in France, or somewhere else, we can find ourselves as happy, or almost as happy, as we were before. You are – so I flatter myself, Eugénie – as convinced as it is possible to be that your mother is the sole cause of all our misfortunes; you know that I have not lost sight of my vengeance: if I have disguised it from my wife, you have learnt the reasons for it, you have applauded them, you have helped me to fashion the blind-fold which I prudently tied round her eyes. We have reached the appointed time, Eugénie; we must act; your security depends on it; what you are about to undertake will ensure my security once and for all; you will understand me, I hope, and you are too intelligent for what I am about to propose to be alarmed even for a moment by it... Yes, my daughter, we must act, act without delay, act without remorse, and this must be your doing. Your mother has tried to make you unhappy, she has sullied the bond she claims to have with you, she has lost any right to it: from that moment on, not only can she no longer be for you anything more than an ordinary woman, but she even becomes your most deadly enemy. Now the law of Nature most intimately engraved in our souls is this: we must be the first to rid ourselves, if we can, of those who conspire against us; this sacred law, which directs and inspires us ceaselessly, did not set within us love of our neighbour before the love which we owe ourselves... We come first, and others only after – that is the way Nature works: no respect for others, consequently, and no indulgence for them once they have proved that our misfortune or our ruin was the sole object of their wishes

— to behave any differently, my daughter, would be to prefer others to ourselves, and that would be absurd. Now, let us get down to the reasons that must impel the action I am advising you to undertake.

"I am obliged to go away; you know why: if I leave you with that woman, then before a month is out, won over by her mother, she will take you back to Paris, and as you can no longer count on being married after the scandal that has just occurred, you can be sure that those two cruel persons will get the upper hand and force you to bewail eternally in a convent both your weakness and our pleasures. It is your grandmother, Eugénie, who is pursuing me, it is she who is joining forces with my enemies to crush me once and for all: can such manoeuvres on her part have any other object than getting you back in her clutches, and can she have you without locking you up? The more my affairs worsen, the more the party that is bent on tormenting us will gain in strength and credit. Now you must not doubt but that your mother is secretly at the head of that party, you must not doubt but that she will join it the minute I am absent. However, this party seeks my ruin only so as to make you the unhappiest of women: we must therefore make haste to subdue it, and we will rob it of its main source of strength if we rob it of Mme de Franval. Is there any other arrangement we can make? If I take you away with me, your mother, enraged, will instantly join her mother, and from that moment, Eugénie, there will be not a moment's peace for us: we will be sought and pursued everywhere; no country will have the right to give us shelter, not a refuge on the earth's surface will be sacred, or inviolable, in the eyes of the monsters whose rage will pursue us; are you unaware of just how far those odious weapons of despotism and tyranny can reach when they are paid for in solid gold coin, and directed by malice? Once your mother is dead, on the other hand, Mme de Farneille, who loves her more than you, and whose every action is on her behalf, seeing her party deprived of the sole person who really ties her to that party, will drop everything, and no longer rouse up my enemies... no longer inflame them against me. From then on, there are two possibilities: either the Valmont business will be settled and nothing can stand in the way of our return to Paris; or it takes a turn for the worse and, forced then to go abroad, at least we are safe from the darts of old Mme de Farneille who, so long as your mother lives, will be intent only on our ruin, because, once again, she imagines that her daughter's happiness can only be secured by our downfall.

"So, from whatever angle you envisage our position, you will see Mme de Franval everywhere blocking the path to our peace of mind, and her hateful existence will appear as the most certain obstacle to our happiness.

"Eugénie, Eugénie," continued Franval energetically, taking both his daughter's hands into his... "dear Eugénie, you love me: so do you want, for fear of taking a step... that is so essential to our interests, to lose for ever the man who adores you? Oh dear and tender friend! Make your mind up; you cannot have it both ways. You are inevitably going to kill one of your parents; the only choice left to you is that of which heart your criminal daggers must pierce: either your mother must perish, or you must renounce me… What am I saying? You must actually slay me… Could I live, alas, without you?… Do you think it would be possible for me to live without my Eugénie? Will I resist the memory of the pleasures I have tasted in your arms… those delightful pleasures, now eternally lost to my senses? Your crime, Eugénie, is the same in both cases: either you must destroy a mother who abhors you and who lives for your unhappiness alone, or you must murder a father who draws breath only for you. So, Eugénie: choose, choose, and if it is I you condemn, do not hesitate, ungrateful daughter; pitilessly tear apart this heart whose sole fault is to have loved too much: I will bless the blows struck by your hand, and my last breath will be a sigh of adoration for you."

Franval stopped, waiting to hear his daughter's reply, but she seemed held in suspense, deep in thought… Finally, she flung herself into her father's arms.

"O you whom I will love all my life long!" she cried. "Can you doubt the choice I will make? Do you suspect that I lack courage? Put weapons in my hands this minute, and the woman who stands condemned both by the horrors she has committed and by the need for your security will soon fall beneath my blows. Instruct me, Franval, give me

my rules of conduct, then leave, as your safety requires...
I will act during your absence, I will keep you informed
about everything, but however things turn out... once our
enemy has been destroyed, I demand that you do not leave
me alone in this chateau... Come and fetch me, or let me
know where I can join you."

"Beloved daughter," said Franval, embracing the monster
he had seduced all too well, "I well knew that I would find in
you all the sentiments of love and firmness necessary to our
mutual happiness... Take this box... Death lies within it."

Eugénie took the fatal box, she repeated the oaths she
had sworn to her father; their other plans were settled: they
arranged that she would await the outcome of the trial, and
depending on whether the judge decided for or against her
father, the planned crime would take place, or not... They
separated; Franval went to find his wife, he took audacity
and hypocrisy so far as to drown her in tears, and to receive,
without belying himself, the touching and innocent caresses
lavished on him by that angel of heaven. Then, having agreed
that she would remain in Alsace with her daughter, whatever
the outcome of his trial, the villain got on his horse and rode
away... away from the innocence and virtue that he had for
so long besmirched by his crimes.

Franval went to take up residence in Basel, so as to ensure
that he would be safe from any prosecution that might be
set in motion against him and, at the same time, to be as
close to Valmor as possible, so that his letters could, during

his absence, sustain in Eugénie the frame of mind he wished in her... It was about twenty-five leagues from Basel to Valmor: but communications between the two places were easy enough – even though they necessitated passing right through the middle of the Black Forest – for him to manage to receive news from his daughter once a week. As a precaution, Franval had taken immense sums of money with him, but more in paper bills than in silver.

Let us leave him to take up residence in Switzerland, and let us return to his wife. There was nothing as pure or sincere as the intentions of this excellent creature; she had promised her husband she would remain in the country until she received further orders from him; as she assured Eugénie every day, nothing would have made her change her resolution... Unfortunately, far from placing in her mother the trust that this worthy person should have inspired her with, and still persuaded by the unjust views of Franval, who nursed the seeds of her prejudice by regular letters, Eugénie could not imagine she had a worse enemy in the world than her mother. And yet there was nothing her mother did not do to overcome in her daughter the insuperable alienation which that ungrateful girl continued to feel in the depths of her heart. She overwhelmed her with caresses and the marks of friendship, she tenderly looked forward with her to the safe return of her husband, and sometimes went so far in sweetness and graciousness as to thank Eugénie and attribute all the merit for this happy conversion to her; then she would express sorrow at having become the innocent cause of the new misfortunes menacing Franval: far from accusing Eugénie of them, she blamed herself alone, and pressing her to her breast, she humbly asked her, with tears in her eyes, if she would ever be able to forgive her... Eugénie's execrable soul resisted these angelic overtures; that perverse soul could no longer hear the voice of Nature: vice had closed all the roads that might have enabled it to reach her... Withdrawing coldly from her mother's arms, she gazed at her with eyes that were at times distraught, and told herself, as if to urge herself on: "How false this woman is... how treacherous!... She caressed me just like this on the day she had me abducted." But these unjust reproaches were merely the abominable sophistries with which crime props itself up when it is seeking to stifle the voice of duty. Mme de Franval, who had agreed to the abduction of Eugénie in the hope that it would bring happiness to her daughter... and peace of mind to herself, and who had been impelled by virtue alone, had been able to disguise the steps she had taken: pretence of this kind is frowned on only by the guilty man it deceives; it does not offend against probity. So Eugénie resisted all the tenderness of Mme de Franval, because she wanted to commit a horrendous crime, and not because of the misdeeds of a mother who had certainly done nothing wrong to her daughter.

Towards the end of the first month of their stay in Valmor, Mme de Farneille wrote to her daughter that the investigation into her husband's actions had taken an extremely serious turn and, given the fear of a humiliating arrest, the return of Mme de Franval and Eugénie was becoming absolutely necessary – both to make a good impression on the public, whose tongue was wagging most spitefully, and also so that the three of them might be reunited – and thus try to reach an arrangement which would appease justice, and deal with the guilty man without condemning him to death.

Mme de Franval, who had resolved to keep nothing hidden from her daughter, immediately showed her this letter. Eugénie, fixing her mother with a cool stare, asked what action she thought it best to take, given this sad news.

"I do not know," replied Mme de Franval... "If you think about it, what good are we doing here? Would we not be a thousand times more useful to my husband, if we followed my mother's advice?"

"You are the mistress, madam," replied Eugénie, "I am here to obey you, and my submission to you is assured..."

But Mme de Franval, clearly seeing from the dryness of her answer that this choice of action did not suit her daughter, told her that she would wait a little longer, that she would write back, and that Eugénie could be sure that, if she deviated from Franval's intentions, it would only be if she was absolutely certain that she would be more useful to him in Paris than in Valmor.

Another month went by in this way, during which Franval did not stop writing to his wife and his daughter, and receiving from them letters that were as if designed to be agreeable to him, since in the one set he saw nothing but a perfect compliance with his desires, and in the other nothing but the firmest and most entire resolve to carry out the planned crime, as soon as the development of the investigation required it, or as soon as Mme de Franval seemed to yield to her mother's requests. "For," Eugénie said in her letters, "if I cannot see in your wife anything but uprightness and sincerity, and if the friends who are serving your interests in the investigations in Paris succeed in bringing things to a successful conclusion, I will hand over to you the task you entrusted to me, and you can carry it out yourself when we are together, if you still think it suitable, unless, that is, in either case, you order me to take action, and find it indispensable for me to do so; then I will take it all on myself, you may rest assured."

Franval replied saying that he approved of all his daughter had told him, and this was the last letter he received from her and the last he wrote. After this, the post brought no more letters. Franval started to worry; when the next delivery brought him no more relief, he fell into despair, and as his natural agitation did not allow him to wait any longer, he straight away decided to come to Valmor himself to find out the reasons for the delay that was causing him such cruel anxiety.

He mounted his horse, followed by a faithful manservant. He was to arrive on the second day, too late at night to be recognized by anybody. At the entrance to the woods which surround the chateau of Valmor and extend as far as the Black Forest to the east, six heavily armed men stopped Franval and his lackey; they requested his purse: these rogues were well informed, they knew who they were talking to, they knew that Franval, implicated in an investigation that was looking bad for him, never went out without his wallet and a huge sum of money... The manservant put up a fight, and was soon stretched out lifeless on the ground next to his horse; Franval, sword in hand, leapt to the ground, charged at those wretches, wounded three of them and found himself surrounded by the others. He was relieved of all his possessions, although they could not wrest his weapon from him, and the robbers made their escape as soon as they had stripped him. Franval pursued them, but the robbers, riding like the wind with their booty and their horses, vanished, and it was soon impossible to know in which direction they had sped.

It was a terrifying night: the north wind, the hail... all the elements seemed to have been unleashed against this wretched man... There are perhaps cases where Nature, revolted by the crimes of the man she is pursuing, seeks to visit upon him, before drawing him to her, all the afflictions at her disposal... Franval, half-naked, but still gripping his sword, made his way as best he could from that fateful spot, heading in the direction of Valmor. As he did not know the area surrounding a property where he had been only on that one occasion in which we have seen him there, he was soon lost on the dark roads of that forest which was completely unknown to him... Quite exhausted, prostrate with grief... consumed by anxiety, tormented by the storm, he threw himself to the ground, and there, the first tears he had ever shed in his life flooded from his eyes...

"Unfortunate man that I am!" he exclaimed. "So everything is finally conspiring to crush me... to make me feel remorse!... It was by the hand of misfortune that remorse was to penetrate my soul: lulled by the balm of prosperity, I would never have experienced it. Oh you, whom I so grievously outraged, you, who perhaps at this moment are falling victim to my fury and barbarity... adorable wife... might it be that the world, made glorious by your existence, still possesses you? Has the hand of Heaven put a stop to my horrid deeds?... Eugénie! A daughter too ready to trust me... too unworthily seduced by my abominable subterfuges... has Nature softened your heart?... Has it arrested the cruel effects of my influence and your weakness? Is there still time?... Is there still time, just heavens?"

All at once, the mournful and majestic sound of several church bells, ringing out dolefully towards the clouds, added to the horror of his fate... He was filled with fear and alarm...

"What do I hear?" he cried, rising to his feet... "Barbarous girl... is it death?... Is it vengeance?... Is it the Furies of hell coming to complete their work?... What are these sounds telling me?... Where am I? Can I really hear them?... O

97

Heaven, complete, complete your chastisement of this guilty man!..."

And, falling prostrate, he continued:

"Great God! Suffer me to add my voice to those that are imploring you at this moment... Look on my remorse and your power... Forgive me for having failed to acknowledge you... and condescend to grant my wishes... the first wishes I dare to send up to you!... Supreme Being... preserve virtue, safeguard the woman who was your most beautiful image in this world; may these sounds, alas, may these melancholy sounds not be the ones I fear!"

Franval, at his wits' end... no longer knowing what he was doing, nor where he was going, uttering disjointed words, followed the path that he had come across... He heard someone... He came back to his senses... He pricked up his ears... It was a man on horseback...

"Whoever you may be," exclaimed Franval, advancing towards the man... "whoever you may be, have pity on a wretch driven to distraction by suffering! I am ready to lay hands on my own life... Lead me, help me, if you are a soul and capable of compassion... save me from myself, I beg you!"

"Good God!" replied a voice that this wretched man knew all too well. "What! You, here?... Heavens above, begone!"

And Clervil – he it was, that worthy mortal who had escaped from the chains laid on him by Franval, and was now sent by Fate to that unhappy man at the most dismal moment of his life – Clervil leapt from his horse and came and fell into the arms of his enemy.

"Is it you, monsieur," said Franval, pressing that honest man to his breast, "is it you, the man against whom, as my conscience reproaches me, I have committed so many foul deeds?"

"Calm yourself, monsieur, calm yourself; I have put behind me the misfortunes that so recently overwhelmed me; I no longer remember those you tried to inflict on me, now that Heaven is allowing me to be of use to you... and that is what I intend to be, monsieur, in a manner that is doubtless cruel, but necessary... Let us sit down... let us rest at the foot of this cypress, only its sinister leaves can constitute a suitable wreath for you now... Oh my dear Franval, how many disasters I must tell you of!... Weep... Oh my dear friend! Tears can give you relief, and I will have to draw even bitterer tears from your eyes... They are gone, the days of delight... they have vanished for you like a dream: only days of suffering are left."

"Oh! Monsieur, I understand... those church bells..."

"They are bearing to the feet of the Supreme Being... the homage, the prayers of the sorrowing inhabitants of Valmor, whom the Eternal did not allow to know an angel but to pity her and mourn her loss..."

Then Franval, turning the point of his sword against this heart, was about to sever the thread of his days, but Clervil, preventing that act of fury, cried:

"No, no, my friend, dying is not the answer, you must rather make reparation. Listen to me, I have much to say to you, you need to be calm to hear it."

"Very well, monsieur. Speak! I am listening; thrust the dagger by slow degrees into my heart. It is only just that it be oppressed in the same way that it has sought to torment others."

"I will be brief as regards myself, monsieur," said Clervil. "After several months in the dreadful place you had locked me away in, I was fortunate enough to move my jailer to pity. He opened the door; I impressed·on him the need above all to conceal with the greatest care the injustice you had permitted yourself to commit against me. He will not speak of it, dear Franval, he will never speak of it."

"Oh, Monsieur!…"

"Listen to me; as I have said, I have many other things to tell you. Once back in Paris, I learnt of your unfortunate venture… your departure… I shared the tears of Mme de Farneille… they were more sincere than you had believed. I joined forces with that worthy woman to persuade Mme de Franval to bring Eugénie back to us, their presence being more necessary in Paris than Alsace… You had forbidden her to leave Valmor… She obeyed… She transmitted those orders to us, she told us of her extreme reluctance to transgress them; she tarried for as long as she could… You were found guilty, Franval… and guilty you are. Your head is forfeit for the crime of murder on the highways: neither the pleading of Mme de

Farneille, nor the steps taken by your friends and relations have managed to turn away the sword of justice: you have fallen prey to it... your name is tarnished for ever... you are ruined... all your belongings have been seized..." And seeing Franval make a second impulsive and furious gesture: "Listen to me, monsieur, listen to me, I demand it as a reparation for your crimes; I demand it in the name of the Heaven that your repentance may still appease. We immediately wrote to Mme de Franval and informed her of everything: her mother told her that her presence had become indispensable, and she was sending me to Valmor to impress on her the urgent necessity of leaving: I followed the letter, but unfortunately it arrived before me; it was too late when I arrived... Your horrible plot had succeeded all too well; I found Mme de Franval dying... Oh, monsieur! What villainy!... But I am touched to see you in such a state, I will cease to reproach you for your crimes... You must know everything: Eugénie could not withstand this spectacle; her repentance, when I arrived, was already finding expression in tears and the most bitter sobs... Oh, monsieur! How can I describe to you the cruel effect of these different scenes!... Your wife expiring... her face wracked by convulsions of pain... Eugénie, restored to nature, screaming pitifully, confessing her guilt, calling on death, trying to do away with herself, one minute falling to the feet of those she was imploring, the next pressed tight to her mother's breast, seeking to revive her with her own breath, warm her with her tears and soften her with her

remorse: such, monsieur, were the dismal sights that met my
eyes when I entered your house. Mme de Franval recognized
me... she pressed my hands... shed her tears on them and
uttered a few words that I found it difficult to hear: they
barely emerged from that breast choked by the palpitations
brought on by the poison... She found excuses for you...
she implored Heaven on your behalf... she asked especially
for mercy on her daughter... You can see, barbarous man,
how the last thoughts and last prayers of the woman whose
heart you broke were even now aimed at your happiness! I
did everything I could, I roused the domestic servants to do
likewise, I employed the services of the most celebrated spe-
cialists... I showered consolations on your Eugénie; touched
by the dreadful state she was in, I did not feel I could refuse
them to her. Nothing had any effect: your unfortunate wife
gave up her soul in shudders and torments impossible to
describe... At this fateful moment, monsieur, I observed
one of the sudden effects of remorse that I had never experienced up until then: Eugénie flung herself on her mother
and died at the same time as she did. We thought she had
merely swooned... No, all her faculties were extinguished;
her organs, absorbed by the shock of the situation, had all
seized up at the same time, she had really expired under the
violent blow of remorse, sorrow and despair... Yes, monsieur,
they are both lost and gone for you, and those church bells,
the tolling of which still strikes your ears, are celebrating two
creatures at once, born one of the other for your happiness,

whom your misdeeds turned into victims of their affection for you, and whose bloody images will pursue you into the darkness of the grave.

"Oh dear Franval! Was I wrong when, not so long ago, I urged you to climb out of the abyss into which your passions were dragging you, and will you now ridicule and carp at the disciples of virtue? Will they be wrong, henceforth, to worship at virtue's altars, when they see at crime's door so much distress and so many afflictions?"

Clervil stopped. He gazed at Franval; he saw that he was dumbstruck with sorrow; his eyes were staring fixedly ahead, tears were flowing from them, but his lips were unable to express a single word. Clervil asked him the reasons for the state of nakedness in which he found him: Franval told him briefly.

"Ah, monsieur!" that generous mortal exclaimed. "How happy I am, even amidst the horrors that surround me, to be able at least to bring you some relief! I was going to find you in Basel, I was going to tell you everything, I was going to offer you the little that I possess... Accept it, I beg you: I am not rich, as you know... but here are a hundred louis... my savings, all that I have... I insist..."

"What a generous man you are!" exclaimed Franval, clasping the knees of that honest and rare friend. "To me?... Heavens above! Do I need help after the losses I have suffered! And it is you... you, that I have treated so badly... it is you who come running to help me?"

"Should we remember insults and injuries when misfortune overwhelms the man who inflicted them on us? The vengeance we owe him, in such a case, is that of bringing him relief: and what is the point of pouring more accusations on him, when his own self-reproaches are rending his heart?... Monsieur, this is the voice of Nature: you can see clearly that the sacred worship of a Supreme Being does not run contrary to it as you imagined, since the counsels inspired by the former are merely the sacred laws of the latter."

"No," replied Franval, rising to his feet, "no, monsieur, I no longer have need of anything: Heaven, leaving me this last possession," he continued, indicating his sword, "teaches me the use to which I should put it..." And, gazing at his sword: "It is the same weapon, yes, my dear and only friend, it is the same weapon which my angelic wife seized one day to pierce her breast with, when I was pouring horror and slander on her... it is the same... I might perhaps find traces of her sacred blood on it... My own blood must efface them... Let us be going... let us find some cottage where I can communicate to you my last will and testament... and then we will bid each other farewell for ever..."

They walked on; they looked for a path that would bring them to some dwelling place... Night continued to envelop the forest in its thick veils... doleful chants could be heard, the pallid flicker of a few torches suddenly dispersed the darkness, casting a dismal hue that only sensitive souls can conceive of; the tolling of the bells broke out twice as loud and mingled with those gloomy accents, which could still barely be made out; thunder and lightning, silent up until now, blazed across the sky, and added its crash to the funereal sounds that could be heard. The lightning furrowing the clouds, intermittently eclipsing the sinister flame of the torches, seemed to be trying to wrest from the inhabitants of earth the right to conduct to her burial the woman that this cortège was bearing along: everything inspired horror, everything breathed desolation… It seemed that Nature had been plunged into eternal mourning.

"What is this?" asked Franval in agitation.

"Nothing," replied Clervil, grasping his friend by the hand, and leading him away from that road.

"Nothing? You are not telling me the truth, I want to see what it is…"

He rushed forward… he saw a coffin.

"Just Heavens!" he exclaimed. "Look, it is her… it is her! God is permitting me to see her again…"

At the bidding of Clervil, who could see it was impossible to calm this wretched man, the priests silently withdrew… Franval, frantic, flung himself onto the coffin, and pulled from it the sad remains of the woman he had so deeply insulted; he seized her body in his arms, placed it at the foot of a tree and, throwing himself upon it with all the madness of despair, cried, beside himself:

"Oh you whose life has been extinguished by my barbarous behaviour, pitiable creature I still idolize, see at your feet your husband making bold to ask you to forgive him and have mercy on him! Do not imagine it is so that I can live on after you, no, no, it is so that the Eternal, moved by your virtues, will deign, if possible, to forgive me as well as you... You must have blood, dear wife, you must have blood to be avenged... and you shall be... Ah! See my tears first, and see my repentance; I am going to follow you, beloved shade... but who will receive my stricken soul, if you do not implore mercy on it? Spurned from God's arms as from your breast, do you want it to be condemned to the dreadful torments of hell, when it repents so sincerely for its crimes?... Forgive, dear soul, forgive me for them, and see how I avenge them."

At these words, Franval, eluding the eyes of Clervil, thrust the sword he was holding twice through his body; his impure blood flowed onto his victim and seemed to sully her much more than it avenged her.

"Oh my friend!" he said to Clervil. "I die, but I die in the bosom of remorse... Inform those who are still left to me of my deplorable end and my crimes; tell them that this is the way the wretched slave of his passions must die, when he is vile enough to have stifled in his own heart the outcry of duty and Nature. Do not refuse my desire to share the coffin of my unhappy wife: I would not have deserved it without my remorse, but that remorse renders me worthy of it, and I demand it – farewell."

Clervil granted the wishes of that unfortunate man. The cortège resumed its progress; an eternal resting place soon buried for ever a husband and wife born to love one another, and made for happiness, and who would have been able to enjoy happiness alone, if crime and its fearful disorders, committed by the guilty hand of one of them, had not changed all the roses of their life into serpents.

The honest priest soon relayed to Paris the dreadful details of these diverse catastrophes. No one showed any surprise at the death of Franval: it was only his life that had been a cause of vexation; but his wife was mourned... deeply and bitterly: and what creature, after all, is more precious, more attractive in the eyes of men, than the woman who has cherished, respected and cultivated all earthly virtues, only to find, at every step, both misfortune and sorrow?

Note on the Text

The edition used is from the *Œuvres complètes du Marquis de Sade* (Paris: Société Nouvelle des Editions Pauvert, 1986), incorporating material discovered by Maurice Heine and published in 1933. I have consulted with great profit the translation by Margaret Crosland: *Eugénie de Franval and Other Stories* (London: Neville Spearman, 1965).

ALMA CLASSICS

ALMA CLASSICS aims to publish mainstream and lesser-known European classics in an innovative and striking way, while employing the highest editorial and production standards. By way of a unique approach the range offers much more, both visually and textually, than readers have come to expect from contemporary classics publishing.

～

1. James Hanley, *Boy*
2. D.H. Lawrence, *The First Women in Love*
3. Charlotte Brontë, *Jane Eyre*
4. Jane Austen, *Pride and Prejudice*
5. Emily Brontë, *Wuthering Heights*
6. Anton Chekhov, *Sakhalin Island*
7. Giuseppe Gioacchino Belli, *Sonnets*
8. Jack Kerouac, *Beat Generation*
9. Charles Dickens, *Great Expectations*
10. Jane Austen, *Emma*
11. Wilkie Collins, *The Moonstone*
12. D.H. Lawrence, *The Second Lady Chatterley's Lover*
13. Jonathan Swift, *The Benefit of Farting Explained*
14. Anonymous, *Dirty Limericks*
15. Henry Miller, *The World of Sex*
16. Jeremias Gotthelf, *The Black Spider*
17. Oscar Wilde, *The Picture Of Dorian Gray*
18. Erasmus, *Praise of Folly*
19. Henry Miller, *Quiet Days in Clichy*
20. Cecco Angiolieri, *Sonnets*
21. Fyodor Dostoevsky, *Humiliated and Insulted*
22. Jane Austen, *Sense and Sensibility*
23. Theodor Storm, *Immensee*
24. Ugo Foscolo, *Sepulchres*
25. Boileau, *Art of Poetry*
26. Georg Kaiser, *Plays Vol. 1*
27. Émile Zola, *Ladies' Delight*
28. D.H. Lawrence, *Selected Letters*
29. Alexander Pope, *The Art of Sinking in Poetry*
30. E.T.A. Hoffmann, *The King's Bride*
31. Ann Radcliffe, *The Italian*
32. Prosper Mérimée, *A Slight Misunderstanding*
33. Giacomo Leopardi, *Canti*
34. Giovanni Boccaccio, *Decameron*
35. Annette von Droste-Hülshoff, *The Jew's Beech*
36. Stendhal, *Life of Rossini*
37. Eduard Mörike, *Mozart's Journey to Prague*
38. Jane Austen, *Love and Friendship*
39. Leo Tolstoy, *Anna Karenina*
40. Ivan Bunin, *Dark Avenues*
41. Nathaniel Hawthorne, *The Scarlet Letter*

42. Sadeq Hedayat, *Three Drops of Blood*
43. Alexander Trocchi, *Young Adam*
44. Oscar Wilde, *The Decay of Lying*
45. Mikhail Bulgakov, *The Master and Margarita*
46. Sadeq Hedayat, *The Blind Owl*
47. Alain Robbe-Grillet, *Jealousy*
48. Marguerite Duras, *Moderato Cantabile*
49. Raymond Roussel, *Locus Solus*
50. Alain Robbe-Grillet, *In the Labyrinth*
51. Daniel Defoe, *Robinson Crusoe*
52. Robert Louis Stevenson, *Treasure Island*
53. Ivan Bunin, *The Village*
54. Alain Robbe-Grillet, *The Voyeur*
55. Franz Kafka, *Dearest Father*
56. Geoffrey Chaucer, *Canterbury Tales*
57. Ambrose Bierce, *The Monk and the Hangman's Daughter*
58. Fyodor Dostoevsky, *Winter Notes on Summer Impressions*
59. Bram Stoker, *Dracula*
60. Mary Shelley, *Frankenstein*
61. Johann Wolfgang von Goethe, *Elective Affinities*
62. Marguerite Duras, *The Sailor from Gibraltar*
63. Robert Graves, *Lars Porsena*
64. Napoleon Bonaparte, *Aphorisms and Thoughts*
65. Joseph von Eichendorff, *Memoirs of a Good-for-Nothing*
66. Adelbert von Chamisso, *Peter Schlemihl*
67. Pedro Antonio de Alarcón, *The Three-Cornered Hat*
68. Jane Austen, *Persuasion*
69. Dante Alighieri, *Rime*
70. Anton Chekhov, *The Woman in the Case and Other Stories*
71. Mark Twain, *The Diaries of Adam and Eve*
72. Jonathan Swift, *Gulliver's Travels*
73. Joseph Conrad, *Heart of Darkness*
74. Gottfried Keller, *A Village Romeo and Juliet*
75. Raymond Queneau, *Exercises in Style*
76. Georg Büchner, *Lenz*
77. Giovanni Boccaccio, *Life of Dante*
78. Jane Austen, *Mansfield Park*
79. E.T.A. Hoffmann, *The Devil's Elixirs*
80. Claude Simon, *The Flanders Road*
81. Raymond Queneau, *The Flight of Icarus*
82. Niccolò Machiavelli, *The Prince*
83. Mikhail Lermontov, *A Hero of our Time*
84. Henry Miller, *Black Spring*
85. Victor Hugo, *The Last Day of a Condemned Man*
86. D.H. Lawrence, *Paul Morel*
87. Mikhail Bulgakov, *The Life of Monsieur de Molière*
88. Leo Tolstoy, *Three Novellas*
89. Stendhal, *Travels in the South of France*
90. Wilkie Collins, *The Woman in White*
91. Alain Robbe-Grillet, *Erasers*
92. Iginio Ugo Tarchetti, *Fosca*
93. D.H. Lawrence, *The Fox*
94. Borys Conrad, *My Father Joseph Conrad*
95. James De Mille, *A Strange Manuscript Found in a Copper Cylinder*
96. Émile Zola, *Dead Men Tell No Tales*

97. Alexander Pushkin, *Ruslan and Lyudmila*
98. Lewis Carroll, *Alice's Adventures Under Ground*
99. James Hanley, *The Closed Harbour*
100. Thomas De Quincey, *On Murder Considered as One of the Fine Arts*
101. Jonathan Swift, *The Wonderful Wonder of Wonders*
102. Petronius, *Satyricon*
103. Louis-Ferdinand Céline, *Death on Credit*
104. Jane Austen, *Northanger Abbey*
105. W.B. Yeats, *Selected Poems*
106. Antonin Artaud, *The Theatre and Its Double*
107. Louis-Ferdinand Céline, *Journey to the End of the Night*
108. Ford Madox Ford, *The Good Soldier*
109. Leo Tolstoy, *Childhood, Boyhood, Youth*
110. Guido Cavalcanti, *Complete Poems*
111. Charles Dickens, *Hard Times*
112. Charles Baudelaire and Théophile Gautier, *Hashish, Wine, Opium*
113. Charles Dickens, *Haunted House*
114. Ivan Turgenev, *Fathers and Children*
115. Dante Alighieri, *Inferno*
116. Gustave Flaubert, *Madame Bovary*
117. Alexander Trocchi, *Man at Leisure*
118. Alexander Pushkin, *Boris Godunov and Little Tragedies*
119. Miguel de Cervantes, *Don Quixote*
120. Mark Twain, *Huckleberry Finn*
121. Charles Baudelaire, *Paris Spleen*
122. Fyodor Dostoevsky, *The Idiot*
123. René de Chateaubriand, *Atala and René*
124. Mikhail Bulgakov, *Diaboliad*
125. Goerge Eliot, *Middlemarch*
126. Edmondo De Amicis, *Constantinople*
127. Petrarch, *Secretum*
128. Johann Wolfgang von Goethe, *The Sorrows of Young Werther*
129. Alexander Pushkin, *Eugene Onegin*
130. Fyodor Dostoevsky, *Notes from Underground*
131. Luigi Pirandello, *Plays Vol. 1*
132. Jules Renard, *Histoires Naturelles*
133. Gustave Flaubert, *The Dictionary of Received Ideas*
134. Charles Dickens, *The Life of Our Lord*
135. D.H. Lawrence, *The Lost Girl*
136. Benjamin Constant, *The Red Notebook*
137. Raymond Queneau, *We Always Treat Women too Well*
138. Alexander Trocchi, *Cain's Book*
139. Raymond Roussel, *Impressions of Africa*
140. Llewelyn Powys, *A Struggle for Life*
141. Nikolai Gogol, *How the Two Ivans Quarrelled*
142. F. Scott Fitzgerald, *The Great Gatsby*
143. Jonathan Swift, *Directions to Servants*
144. Dante Alighieri, *Purgatory*
145. Mikhail Bulgakov, *A Young Doctor's Notebook*
146. Sergei Dovlatov, *The Suitcase*
147. Leo Tolstoy, *Hadji Murat*
148. Jonathan Swift, *The Battle of the Books*
149. F. Scott Fitzgerald, *Tender Is the Night*
150. Alexander Pushkin, *The Queen of Spades and Other Short Fiction*
151. Raymond Queneau, *The Sunday of Life*

152. Herman Melville, *Moby Dick*
153. Mikhail Bulgakov, *The Fatal Eggs*
154. Antonia Pozzi, *Poems*
155. Johann Wolfgang von Goethe, *Wilhelm Meister*
156. Anton Chekhov, *The Story of a Nobody*
157. Fyodor Dostoevsky, *Poor People*
158. Leo Tolstoy, *The Death of Ivan Ilyich*
159. Dante Alighieri, *Vita nuova*
160. Arthur Conan Doyle, *The Tragedy of Korosko*
161. Franz Kafka, *Letters to Friends, Family and Editors*
162. Mark Twain, *The Adventures of Tom Sawyer*
163. Erich Fried, *Love Poems*
164. Antonin Artaud, *Selected Works*
165. Charles Dickens, *Oliver Twist*
166. Sergei Dovlatov, *The Zone*
167. Louis-Ferdinand Céline, *Guignol's Band*
168. Mikhail Bulgakov, *A Dog's Heart*
169. Rayner Heppenstall, *The Blaze of Noon*
170. Fyodor Dostoevsky, *The Crocodile*
171. Anton Chekhov, *The Death of a Civil Servant*
172. Georg Kaiser, *Plays Vol. 2*
173. Tristan Tzara, *Seven Dada Manifestos* and *Lampisteries*
174. Frank Wedekind, *The Lulu Plays and Other Sex Tragedies*
175. Frank Wedekind, *Spring Awakening*
176. Fyodor Dostoevsky, *The Gambler*
177. Prosper Mérimée, *The Etruscan Vase and Other Stories*
178. Edgar Allan Poe, *Tales of the Supernatural*
179. Virginia Woolf, *To the Lighthouse*
180. F. Scott Fitzgerald, *The Beautiful and Damned*
181. James Joyce, *Dubliners*
182. Alexander Pushkin, *The Captain's Daughter*
183. Sherwood Anderson, *Winesburg Ohio*
184. James Joyce, *Ulysses*
185. Ivan Turgenev, *Faust*
186. Virginia Woolf, *Mrs Dalloway*
187. Paul Scarron, *The Comical Romance*
188. Sergei Dovlatov, *Pushkin Hills*
189. F. Scott Fitzgerald, *This Side of Paradise*
190. Alexander Pushkin, *Complete Lyrical Poems*
191. Luigi Pirandello, *Plays Vol. 2*
192. Ivan Turgenev, *Rudin*
193. Raymond Radiguet, *Cheeks on Fire*
194. Vladimir Odoevsky, *Two Days in the Life of the Terrestrial Globe*
195. Copi, *Four Plays*
196. Iginio Ugo Tarchetti, *Fantastic Tales*
197. Louis-Ferdinand Céline, *London Bridge*
198. Mikhail Bulgakov, *The White Guard*
199. George Bernard Shaw, *The Intelligent Woman's Guide*
200. Charles Dickens, *Supernatural Short Stories*
201. Dante Alighieri, *The Divine Comedy*

To order any of our titles and for up-to-date information about our
current and forthcoming publications, please visit our website at:

www.almaclassics.com